...stable

Series

The Secondment

Simpson Munro

This paperback edition published 2020 by Jasami Publishing Ltd
an imprint of Jasami Publishing Ltd
Glasgow, Scotland
https://jasamipublishingltd.com

ISBN 978-1-913798-25-3

Visit JasamiPublishingLtd.com to read more about all our books and to purchase them. You will also find features, author information and news of any events, also be the first to hear about our new releases.

Acknowledgements

I must acknowledge all those who assisted in the process,
specifically Ian and Catherine as well as Holly and May, who
contributed their talents to my work.

A very special thank you must also go to May for her immense
input and expertise.
Meticulous, yes, brilliant, most certainly.

Illustrator

Holly Richards

Editor

May Winton

Dedication

This book is dedicated to my children and my children's children.

Table of Contents

Prologue

I n the early years' Police Constable Andy Blackmore's sole aim was to complete his probationary period as a police officer in a successful manner and learn as much as he could about his new profession from experienced colleagues he had on the shift that he was allocated to when he arrived at Bankvale Police Office. Bankvale was a world apart from his home patch in the east end of Glasgow. He quickly adapted to the village way of life and became a popular figure with his colleagues and the local community due to his down-to-earth manner that he had brought from the building sites and his no-nonsense approach with the local criminals.

Andy was popular with the ladies and during his early years in the job, he had become involved with Catherine, a nurse at a local hospital. When he became part of a team investigating an enquiry involving members of her family that ended in tragedy, their relationship ended.

While on an enquiry at a local high school he met Susan Berger an old school friend. His relationship with her was to lead Andy into enquiries and secondments to other departments, unheard of given his length of service. As Andy's relationship with Susan deepened disturbing information started to surface about her family, meanwhile, he was trying to cope with his debt-ridden brother who was a friend of the Bergers and the deteriorating health of his mother.

Chapter One

As the bells approached Andy and Susan made their way to the local pub. The place was full of regulars who had secured a ticket to bring in a new year with their family, as well as friends, acquaintances, and strangers. Andy and Susan had seats reserved beside their friends. Large chandeliers from a bygone age hung from the high ceiling complimenting three large arched windows with its frosted and stained glass that leads into the archway giving the lounge bar a unique atmosphere. Patrons had their tickets checked before they entered the lounge by two burly doormen. Large speakers blasted out loud music from the resident rock band. Handshakes and hugs were the order of the evening as Andy and Susan made their way to the table occupied by the boys who were long term mates of Andy's, their girlfriends, and their wives. Andy looked around scanning the lounge as he had always done even before his police days. Many known faces were in this evening. Tables surrounded the dance floor which led to a large standing area at the bar. The access to the ladies' and gents' toilets was getting rather crowded.

At ten o'clock the doors were closed as the pub reached capacity, the only exception would be ticket-holding latecomers, the atmosphere was electric as the clock headed towards midnight. The band belted out cover versions of big rock music hits, the beer pumps were churning out pints of lager and beer. The glass measures on the gantry were going as fast as they could filling glasses with whiskey, brandy, vodka, and everything else that was available. The temperature in the lounge was rising with all the bodies in there. The talk at Andy's table was football and rugby orientated among the guys as the girls were more interested in what was handed out by their menfolk at Christmas. It was obvious what the guys had received as presents as it smelled like the aftershave counter at Boots the Chemist.

"Hey, Susan what did you get at Christmas from Andy and keep it clean," asked Sally.

"A diamond bracelet as you can see" swinging her arm about in the air showing off her glittering gift.

"Oh my god that is stunning, anything else?" asked Sally.

Susan looked over at Andy and he nodded his approval.

"Susan… Tell-all" shouted Grace.

"We are, em…. oh hell where do I start," she said putting her hands on her cheeks.

"Okay, we are living together now, and we are engaged!"

Everyone at the table cheered loudly over the music. Congratulations were the order of the day to Andy and Susan. They should have known better to announce that in the pub with the crowd they sat with.

The band finished Smoke on the Water, a Deep Purple classic, the lead singer took to the microphone, "Ladies and Gentlemen a huge congratulations to Big Andy Blackmore and Miss Susan Berger who have become engaged! So, from us to you guys congratulations on your engagement" and the band went into "You are so Beautiful" the 1974 classic song by Joe Cocker. The table where they sat with their friends were overjoyed with the news that they had finally got together. That announcement cost Andy a round of drinks but to him, it was worth it, he had his girl.

"We are Crash, we have 60 seconds left of this year see you all next year" shouted the lead singer down the microphone.

The big television screen behind the band flickered into life as the clock went into a countdown. The television cameras turned towards Big Ben. Strangely, the pub started to go quiet as the seconds of the old year ticked away. As the bells started to chime welcoming in the New Year, BBC Scotland's Hogmanay show went into full swing only to be drowned out by the cheers in the pub that 1982 had arrived. Bar staff and customers greeted each other with hugs and kisses, strangers hugged and kissed strangers.

Andy turned to Susan and wrapped his arms tightly around her. "Happy New Year Susan I just love you too bits" "and I, you also Andy, Happy New Year" she replied. She said that just in time as the band blasted out "Auld Lang Syne" that sounded like it was being played at a hundred miles an hour, probably not what Mr Burns had intended for his poem, but everyone in the lounge, standing and seated joined in.

In the Blackmore household in the east end, the atmosphere was slightly subdued given recent events.

"Happy New Year Alice," said Ricky as the bells rang out, signalling the New Year in their house.

3

"I hope so Ricky. For you too" she replied in a low voice with her mind elsewhere.

Alice found it strange that he did not attempt to approach her to shake her hand, hug her or even kiss her.

"Happy New Year Mum," whispered Ricky giving his mother a hug and a kiss on her cheek before he sat down.

"Thank you, son and you Alice…. you are so special to me."

The scene was repeated in the Berger household, as Brian and Sandra celebrated the occasion without Susan for the first time since her birth.

"Happy New Year, Brian,"

"You also, if you want to call Sheena that is okay" he replied. There was no sign of affection from him whatsoever as he looked at his wife.

"I shall leave it; she is with June tonight but thank you for the offer" replied Sandra, turning her attention to the Hogmanay Show on the television.

At one o'clock in the morning, with the New Year an hour old it was time to head for home with or without friends, the "bouncers" began the unenviable job of having to clear the pub. The prolonged cry of "Ladies and Gentlemen start drinking up and making your way towards the door please" was the cry from the bouncers "you must have parties to go onto somewhere we are sure, so have we, so goodnight and a Happy New Year" but as everyone knew each other they had an easy task on this occasion as the revellers spilt out onto the street. Patrons drifted off to pre-arranged parties, some stood around looking to be invited to parties, most being unsuccessful, others stood leaning against the exterior wall having had a little too much drink to move. Taxis were at a premium despite their double fares policy after the bells. Having said their goodbyes, Andy and Susan walked slowly back to the flat, arms wrapped around each other and inseparable. As they walked along the road, lights from houses were beaming onto the pavement, sounds of loud music coming from within.

They climbed the well-trodden concrete stairs up to the flat, Susan watched as Andy inserted the key into the lock. "Miss Berger, please be the first to enter our abode this year" requested Andy. As Susan crossed the threshold, he followed her in, and the door closed behind them.

They curled up on the couch each holding a crystal brandy glass.

"Happy New Year Miss Berger."

"Happy New Year to you Mr Blackmore."

"Bedtime?" asked Susan.

"Yes, why not we have to go to your parent's tomorrow."

"Yes, but I want to go see your mum," she said.

Just after midday on the first day of 1982, Andy and Susan drove to the Berger household. Andy being brought up a traditional Scot was armed with whiskey and shortbread. Deep down he was praying that the animosity between him and Brian would be laid to rest for the sake of Susan, deep down he knew there was little chance of that. In his head, Andy always decided not to rise to the bait cast out by Brian, therefore he would remain respectful, he knew he had Sandra onside. The information she had given him about their life was priceless, it would be as a last resort for him to use it.

On their arrival at her parents' house, Susan opened the door and burst into the living room shouting, "Happy New Year, mum and dad".

"Happy New Year darling," said Brian standing up from his chair and hugging his daughter and kissing her cheek. "Happy New Year Susan," said her mum rushing out the kitchen, hugging her tightly.

Andy took the initiative, held out his hand, "Happy New Year Brian" he said in a low voice staring into Brian's eyes "and you Andy" briefly shaking his hand.

"Hey Sandra, you little devil Happy New Year," said Andy almost lifting her off her feet in a bear hug.

"You also," she replied laughing.

"Hey mum behave he is mine" she laughed.

"Yeah.... see if I was thirty years younger you would have competition" replied Sandra jokingly.

"Dinner is on shouldn't be that long, Brian, pour the kids a drink and me one also," said Sandra.

Andy and Susan sat on the couch, opposite Brian as he sat watching the usual New Year television rubbish that only the broadcasters could churn out, repeated programme after repeated programme. The only new thing was the evening news even that had some old news to pad it out to its ten-minute slot.

Andy broke the silence in his usual fashion, "Hey Brian I take it at three o'clock we shall be watching Her Majesty Queen Elizabeth the second of the United Kingdom, Great Britain Northern Ireland and the Commonwealth, Defender of the Faith delivering her speech to the nation."

Brian looked at Andy. "That is at Christmas" he replied in a terse tone.

"Awe Susan…. I missed the Queen's speech this year again," said Andy jokingly.

"When was it on?"

"A week ago,"

"Okay, you missed it then" she replied laughing.

"well ah just thought that" he started to say, as he felt an elbow go deep into his ribs from Susan.

"You thought what Andy?" asked Brian failing to see the funny side.

"Nothing it doesn't matter."

"Right as this is my first New Year here, I shall assist Mrs. Berger in the kitchen," said Andy.

"Good idea and next year we shall make dinner for everyone," said Susan.

"Oh, are you planning to stay there that long," said Brian.

"Dad, no is the answer we intend buying a flat or house together, you know as a couple," she said looking at her father then pausing

"Dad, can we get today over without any crap from you? see your days of ruling over me and mum they are over, new day, New Year, a new beginning. Get used to it" warned Susan staring at her father who was taken aback by Susan's remarks and tone.

Andy returned to the living room having heard the raised voices and looking at both Susan and Brian, asked: "What's going on?"

"Nothing," said Susan as she dipped her eyes avoiding looking at Andy.

"Okay, right, fine, your mum and I were having a cooking moment in there."

"Maybe I should join you both."

"Boiled eggs are not on the menu Susan."

"Cheeky cheeky Andy not a good move" laughed Susan.

"Oh, if you say so."

"I do, now get back in there and help mum."

As he went back into the kitchen Andy stood close to Sandra looking at her. Closing his body down he folded his arms and crossed his legs as he leaned back against the worktop.

"What?" asked Sandra.

"Nothing just watching you cooking, learning from your expertise."

"Andy," she said quietly "You are a tease and, you are my daughter's' fiancée."

"And your point is what Mrs. Berger?" he said with a raised eyebrow.

"Nothing, leave it please."

"Certainly" he replied with a wink and a smile.

"Go and find out what they want for starters please," she said looking into his eyes.

Andy lifted a dishtowel, placed it over his arm like a waiter in a restaurant.

"Okay, I have been elected as head waiter, Soup or Prawn Cocktail for starters."

"Soup for me please," said Susan.

"Same here," said Brian.

"Sandra" Andy called out, "do you have a starter called same here."

"No soup or prawns only" she replied.

"Sorry sir same here is off the menu today," he said with a touch of sarcasm.

"Soup," Brian said aggressively.

"Good to know the New Year has not changed you, soup it is."

"Prawn cocktail for me please Sandra I love prawns! I may have two starters."

"Two starters Andy?"

"Maybe even three."

"How can you have three," said Sandra.

"Soup, Prawns and You" he whispered into her ear then laughing, winding her up.

"You are out of order Andy," she said flustered pushing him out of her way with her elbow and laughing.

"Dinner time" he shouted as he carried through the starters laying them on the table.

Two hours later coffee was on the table, the soup and prawns, the steak pie with its accompaniment of roasted potatoes and mixed vegetables, the lemon meringue pie and ice cream had been devoured. "Brian drinks please," said Sandra.

"Susan what are we doing" asked Andy.

"Well I was thinking of that, we can have a drink here then go see your mum then come back here by taxi."

"And where do you think you will be staying here? Brian asked Andy it will not be in Susan's' room that's for sure."

"Oh, for god's sake Brian do you think they have separate rooms at Andy's?" asked Sandra

"Can I clarify something please?" asked Andy.

"It is no longer Andy's place it is now Andy and Susan's place, or even Susan and Andy's"

"Okay, Brian your turn to get to work," said Andy.

"Two Brandies for Susan and I and a vodka and coke for your good lady."

"There is a bottle of Whisky in my bag so I shall pour one for dad," Andy said to Susan as he rose from the table.

The word 'Dad' did not go astray with anyone as Brian's face reddened with anger.

"I have shortbread also for your mum to wrap herself around."

"Thank you, Andrew" replied Sandra with a broad smile kissing him on his cheek as he laid it on the table beside her.

"Ohhhh.... Andrew, now?" said Susan sarcastically as her mother had used his full name. "You do have your feet under the table right enough."

With Susan and Andy having been served by her father with their Brandies, Sandra having her Vodka and Brian receiving his large glass of Whisky courtesy of Andy, Andy stood and proposed a toast to the health and well-being of everyone present during 1982 and that he was looking forward to spending his life with Susan. Glasses were raised and the contents sipped slowly as Andy sat down beside Susan. Andy knew that deep down Brian was not happy with the situation.

"Andrew, I was thinking, how about you and I having a "clear the air" night out at an exclusive club I belong to," said Brian.

"Well as long as Susan and Sandra can come along and enjoy the evening also that would be great."

"I shall have to think about that" he replied.

Andy immediately locked onto Sandra staring at Brian.

"That is a bit off Brian, not inviting your wife and daughter along," said Sandra pausing.

"Is that the club you and I used to go to?" she inquired.

Brian was seething with anger and did not reply, as he lifted his drink to his lips consuming the remainder of his whisky in one gulp.

Andy knew exactly 'the club' Brian was referring to from what Sandra had told him.

"Fiancée Susan shall we head up and see your future in-laws."

"Yes great."

"Are there any prawns left Sandra."

"Yes."

"Good, prawn cocktail for supper…. see you guys about eleven o'clock?"

"That would be good Andy you two enjoy your evening," said Sandra as she watched them leave the house in search of a taxi.

Within fifteen minutes they were standing at the door of the Blackmore villa awaiting a reply as Susan rang the doorbell.

"Happy New Year Alice and Happy New Year to my very favourite children," said Andy as she opened the door with the kids right behind her.

"Happy New Year to both of you" as they hugged each other.

"Happy New Year Aunty Susan we love you," said Alfie.

"Awe that is so lovely thanks Annie and Alfie and I love you guys also" as she hugged them both.

"Ricky is in the living room," said Alice.

Andy and Susan walked into the living room to see Ricky sitting there watching television, they were followed in by Alice and the children.

"Ricky, Happy New Year," said Andy echoed by Susan.

"Yeah, thanks, to you also" he replied without standing or taking his eyes off the television screen.

Alice nodded to Andy and Susan to follow her into the kitchen which they did.

"Mum, Happy New Year said Andy kissing her cheek and wrapping his arms around her.

"Happy New Year Mrs. B," said Susan.

"You also Susan, and I hear that you two have become engaged."

"Yes, we have and, I love your boy to bits."

"I am so pleased Susan, for you and both of you."

Andy looked at his mother and Susan, it was as if the years had been turned back as his mother remembered everything about them.

"Mum it is New Year what would you like to drink."

"Now let me think, I used to like vodka and orange, but I think a little sherry shall do this year please," she replied being alert to the celebrations.

"Susan I will be back, two minutes," said Andy leaving her with his mother and the children who had returned to the kitchen.

"Alice" Andy beckoned her to the lounge.

"What is going on Alice?" he asked her behind the closed door.

She said that after Ricky got home and after they left yesterday, he seemed distant. She was not happy with his demeanour like everything was distant to him. Andy reminded her that things may not be the same in months or years to come. The carbon monoxide poisoning would have affected him. Alice said she did not know if she was strong enough to cope with the situation with Ricky being the way he was, now unemployed, their mother and having the children.

Alice said that she was worried about something else he had brought up.

"He wanted to know if everything was alright between us especially as you had stayed overnight," said Alice

"What did you say?"

"I told him you could not have been better with me and the kids."

"So, what is the problem?" asked Andy.

"I just don't know at the moment" was her reply.

Andy and Alice returned to the kitchen and there was New Year joy and laughter all around. Andy and his Mum told stories of years gone with the family parties on January 1, with friends and family, some of whom were gone but remembered with fondness, crammed into a room and kitchen flat, being together with the songs of yesteryear. Tony Bennett was the family sing-along with I Left My Heart in San Francisco. Petula Clark, Lulu, and so many more brought in the New Year in times past and of course Motown.

"Where is Ricky?" asked his mother looking around for him.

"I will go get him, mum," said Andy.

"Right you. Shift your butt. Mum is looking for you," Andy said to Ricky.

"Sit down Andy," he asked pointing at the seat opposite.

"What's up Ricky.?

"Do you love Alice and Susan?" asked Ricky, looking directly at Andy

"I am sorry I don't understand that question."

"It doesn't matter, it was just an anonymous phone call I got," he said in an agitated manner and stroking his jaw with his hand

"Ricky talk to me; you have to explain that last question."

"A guy said that while you were here you were with my wife."

"Of course, I was here with your wife and your children looking after them while you lay in a hospital bed" Andy paused, "Ricky… think, please… did you recognise the voice?" he said remaining calm.

"Oh yes, I did."

"Who was it, Ricky?"

"Oh, that is easy it was Brother Berger."

"Do you believe him?"

"Oh yes, he is a brother of mine but not of yours."

"Ricky, listen to me please, your brother Berger is trying to split up Susan and me, did you know that?"

"Maybe so, but why would he want to do that? answer that question, Andy," he asked in a low tone of voice.

"Because he is twisted and evil Ricky that is why."

Ricky sat staring at Andy, "and what makes him wicked and evil Andy"?

"Listen come into the kitchen… please, be with us," asked Andy avoiding his brothers' last question.

"No thank you, Andy" he replied.

Andy went back into the kitchen and sat down. He had to think before speaking to the others in the room.

"Is Ricky coming in Andy?" asked his mother.

"No mum he is tired tonight."

Neither Alice nor Susan believed a word of that. Alice took the kids through to say goodnight to their father. His mum was about to make her way to her flat having had great fun reminiscing.

"Mum come here please."

Andy wrapped his huge arms around her and held her close to him.

"What was that for Andy?"

"New Year mum that's all, you never know if you are going to get another chance to do that."

"Night son," followed by "goodnight Susan," as she made her way out of the kitchen.

A short time later, Alice came back into the kitchen, having put the kids to their beds, she sat down looking exhausted. She rested her elbows on the worktop and rubbed her face with her hands.

"Are you alright Alice?" asked Susan as she was concerned about the way Alice was looking and acting.

"I am exhausted with everything Susan" she paused "Ricky going missing, the debt I just found out about, worrying about the kids, I have had it, Susan I am done in, to be honest," she said as the tears streamed down her face.

"Alice, it is getting late do you want us to stay or will you be alright?" asked Susan as she placed a supporting arm around Alice's' shoulders and pulling her in close.

"I shall be fine; I have to get back to normal," she said as she looked at Andy and pausing, "Anyway, you have done more for me when he was ill and in hospital, than anyone could have I shall always be grateful for that." Said Alice sitting up and wiping the tears from her cheeks taking in a deep breath.

"No problem Alice," said Susan placing her hand on top of Alice's' hand reassuringly.

"Susan you have found yourself an absolute gem."

"Time we headed for the hills I think," said Andy.

"No problem."

"Goodnight Andy and Susan" came from the living room.

"Goodnight Ricky," they replied from the hallway.

Alice closed and locked the large door to the villa and watched as Andy and Susan took the long walk down the driveway and onto the main road. A taxi appeared with its 'begging light' as the locals would say meaning it was for hire. They got in and gave the destination address.

"No problem Andy" then there was silence as the driver stared into the rear-view mirror.

"Long time no see Andy," he said with a smile on his face thinking that he had not been recognised as he drove off with his hires.

Andy stared into the rear-view mirror, looking into the eyes of the driver who knew him by name.

Andy whispered to Susan I am going to ask him to pull over and I shall leave my door open."

"Driver pull over please."

"You sure Andy?"

"Yes, very sure."

"Sorry but it's New Year double fare."

Andy got out with that face on him that trouble was about to erupt. He pulled open the door and dragged the taxi driver out of his vehicle in a split second.

"Gerry, Gerry O'Brien as Andy wrapped his arms around him, how are you mate been so long."

"Christ Andy, I thought you were going to do me,"

"I recognised your eyes in the mirror, then thought he is mine" he laughed.

"Geezuz you are a bam."

"Susan sat dumbfounded not for the first time. "Blackmore" she shouted, "Get back in here and explain and let the guy get to work."

Through the intercom, they told Susan that they had grown up together in the east end and they still had mutual friends in the area and loved winding each other up.

Andy told Gerry on the journey to her parents' house that he and Susan had got engaged.

"You are having a laugh Blackmore, engaged? you must be really special Susan to capture this one, hey Andy, wait until I go home and tell Andrea that one, she will piss herself laughing."

Arriving at their destination the meter was showing the value of the journey. Big man, we have known each other since we were kids. Free ride for you and your lady, but, a wedding invite, please. "Gerry, we have known each other since kids, wedding invite pending, take this and get yourself a drink please, listen tell the boys I will be back here for the stag night and we shall all get together for that night, or two nights or however long it takes," he said laughing looking at Susan.

"Thanks, big man you are a gem"

"You also Gerry."

"Susan" handing her a card. "If you wanna know anything about him gimme a call" as he burst out laughing.

"Will do Gerry," she said.

As Gerry drove away, Susan asked Andy "is there anyone in the east end you don't know?"

"Aye, yer Da' but I am getting there" he replied with a laugh as they made their way along the path to the front door.

Susan and Andy went into the house quietly as they did not know if Brian or Sandra would be awake. The last thing that Andy wanted to do was to confront Brian about the alleged phone call to Ricky. When they opened the living room door they saw that Brian was sitting waiting for them; Sandra was in bed. Susan decided that enough was enough and she would go to bed. Andy said that he would sleep on the couch before Brian got a chance to make an issue of the situation. Brian rose from his chair and poured a whisky for himself and brandy for his guest. He handed Andy his glass and sat down all the time remaining silent. He looked over at Andy, who was sitting to his right on the couch.

"Tell me something what do you know about me?" Brian asked as he looked into his glass which he had held up to eye level as if examining the contents.

"Concerning what?"

"My working and private life."

"Enough."

"What does that mean?" he replied lowering his glass resting in on the arm of his chair.

"Enough to destroy you as you have tried to do to Susan and me, so here is what you are going to do, you are going to phone my brother and apologise for getting things so tragically wrong about the information you gave him about Alice and me because you have absolutely no evidence of anything happening between us" he paused "Secondly, you are going to back off once and for all and be a good boy or I might just get annoyed with you and your friends and you know what that can lead to, don't you? He paused again making sure his message was getting through to Brian, "Finally if you do not stop, I might just suggest to Susan that we should think about emigrating to Canada or Australia, maybe even New Zealand. We can both get jobs there. After I tell her everything you have done, I am sure she will go" said Andy in a very calm manner in a low voice, while looking directly at Brian Berger who took what was being said to him seriously and made him very uncomfortable in his own home.

"You are an evil psychopath Blackmore, they call you the 'Iceberg' but after what you did at the garage you have a vicious evil streak in you, someday you will end up in jail and that is no place for an ex-cop."

Andy sat staring at Brian, "think about what you have just said and remember those words you have just uttered, they may come back to haunt you" said Andy quietly as he watched Brian finish his whisky and leave the room.

Chapter Two

T he following day Susan and Andy left together after brunch with her parents. The atmosphere between Brian and Andy had been tense but for the sake of Sandra and Susan, they were polite to each other. Andy and Susan went shopping for her engagement ring at a store in a lane just off Sauchiehall Street that Andy knew. A single diamond solitaire ring was chosen and purchased. The saleslady asked if they wanted the ring wrapped but Andy took it from her and placed it on the third finger of Susan's left hand.

"Oh, that rarely happens in here congratulations to both of you," said the saleslady with a broad smile on her face.

"Thank you," they both said sealing their engagement with a kiss.

They left the city centre and headed for the flat where they pottered about tidying up after the festive season and getting ready for the New Year together. Susan made tentative steps into asking Andy what he and her father had been discussing after she went to bed. Andy said that they had that "clear the air" chat that her father wanted and hopefully any misunderstandings between them had been cleared up. She said that she was glad about that as they had to get on together or it was going to be awkward in the future. He agreed. That evening Andy looked out his suit, shirt, and tie for his first day with the CID. Shoes were polished highly as normal before they retired to bed for the night.

At eight o'clock the following morning Andy made his first appearance in the Criminal Investigation Department office, as an Acting Detective Constable, reporting, as instructed, to Detective Sergeant Liam Anderson, an officer with a police long service medal already in the bag. Although not the tallest officer in the department standing about five feet ten inches tall and built proportionately there was a manner about him that was commanding but friendly. He knew most of the officers as he had spoken to them either on the telephone or in-person in the past. Detective Sergeant Anderson showed Andy to his desk. "The drawers on the right-hand side are yours. The drawers on the left belong to DC Colin Wright you will be desk sharing with him as you are on opposite shifts. See that pile of unsolved crime reports lying there, they are yours, so sort them out to prioritise them. Update what you have done at the end of the day keep me up to date with your enquiries and we will get on fine. The briefing is at 08.00 hrs each morning, so don't be late"

"Thank you, Sergeant," said Andy politely as he looked at the pile of crime reports awaiting his attention.

"Hey Iceberg, welcome mate," said DC Bobby Russell as he walked into the room, just in time for the morning briefing.

"Thank you, Bobby" replied Andy shaking his hand warmly.

"What is that you have got?" he asked.

"A pile of unsolved crime reports for the new kid," he said.

"Well man, that is what the new starts get on their first day," Bobby said with a wry smile having seen it all before.

"Thanks for saving them up," said Andy laughing.

Bobby Russell had a long-standing reputation as a good and thorough detective officer and one that the intelligence department loved to get information from as he was reliable. His slight frame, crew cut hairstyle and sharp features belied the fact that he was a detective where he was unknown. By his admission, he was not someone who would get a job as a male model given his dishevelled appearance at times. Somehow managed to get through twenty cigarettes a day.

As the rest of the detectives they came in on staggered starts, they all gave Andy a warm welcome as they were aware of his reputation as a good officer as well as being handy in the event of trouble. Detective Constables Danny Williams and Gordon Yardley knew of his reputation but had never worked with Andy and they were intrigued by their new colleague.

Andy spent a couple of hours sorting out the crime reports, telephoning the complainers and updating the backs of the forms. "A few of them seem interesting to say the least," said Andy.

"Oh, in what way Andy?" asked Bobby.

"Well, this big pile of vandalisms for a start."

"That should be a uniform enquiry" replied Bobby.

"Well, I have it now so have to get on with it."

"Then, there are the fires at premises that have been going on for nearly a year," said Andy.

"Probably insurance jobs if you ask me," said Bobby.

"Wonder if the DS would let me potter about with them for a while."

"Potter all you like Andy what you have is going nowhere other than the unsolved file," shouted Danny from over at his desk and shaking his head.

Detective Constable Danny Williams was in his mid-forties, he was by all accounts a runner who liked to keep fit, even though he smoked like a chimney, just like Bobby. His receding hairline and slim build made him another one in the office that did not look like a typical detective. His speciality was initial scenes of crimes examinations.

"Right fine," said Andy holding the bundle of crime reports. This enquiry was going to get a new set of eyes, his!

Detective Constable Gordon Yardley rose from his desk and went over to where Andy was sitting. He sat on the edge of Andy's' desk and looked at him as he laid out each of the crime reports.

"What are you hoping to get out of this secondment Andy?"

"your experience and expertise" he replied

"You won't be here long enough to get all of that" Gordon replied laughing as he made his way back to his desk.

Detective Constable Gordon Yardley was everything the public perceived as a Detective, tall, well built, well dressed, authoritative, with a rough edge that scared even the hardest police officers. He was a fearsome looking individual with a large scar down the side of his face which he got early in his service from the flash of a blade wielded by a gangster in the city.

 After everything that went on over the New Year, Andy was glad to be back at work and the banter that went with it.

"Andy, what is this on the desk?" asked DS Anderson.

"It is little piles of crap that I have neatly sorted out to get a body or two for them."

 "New starts think they know everything," said Anderson shaking his head and walking away.

"Andy, we heard you were a handful," uttered Bobby.

"Bobby, listen, I am not a handful; I am down to earth and truthful some don't like that."

"This should be a fun ride with you here," replied Bobby.

"Hey, big man Happy New Year" came the female voice from behind him.

"Aw magic, Happy New Year June, you also Joe."

"Gimme a kiss you, big hunk," said June.

"June do I get one also?" asked Bobby.

"Dream on" she replied laughing.

"Joe back to the ranch for us great to see you Andy catch up soon." Said June.

"Andy if you want someone to go out with you on enquiries then I can do that as we are going to be on the same shift, you also got Danny and Gordon that will neighbour you,"

"Thank you," said Andy.

Andy felt that his first day was like starting his probation period all over again, and in a way he was. The vandalisms he was given ran into thousands of pounds of damage to people's property especially their cars which were an easy target in the dark of the night. The four fires which caused damage to property ran close to one million pounds but seemed to have been discarded along the way for more important crimes. Then there were the stolen cars ten of them in total most recovered, a few found burned out with a value of just over eighty-five thousand pounds.

"Andy, I have a couple of enquiries I need to get on with if you want to neighbour me"

"Sure, that would be great thanks" as he gathered his baton and handcuffs.

As he hung his handcuffs over his belt pouch, he looked confused as to where he would wear his baton.

"Bobby where do I put this" referring to his baton as everyone in the room burst out laughing.

"Wrong question big man, do you want an answer to that?" was Bobby's reply throwing him a shoulder holster from his drawer.

"Nah, maybe not," said Andy with a smile on his face and a shake of his head realising the stupidity of that question among seasoned detectives.

Later in the day, Bobby took Andy out and about with him as he had a few minor enquiries to round off before writing off the crime reports as unsolved. They discussed Andy's career and what he had been doing in his past life. Turned out Bobby had been a plumber before joining the police fifteen years ago.

"Bobby can we stop off at the newsagents I want to speak to someone there please," asked Andy.

"Sure" replied Bobby.

As Andy went onto the newsagents "Holyeeeee shit" said Jessie "look at you, Andy Blackmore."

"Hi Jessie, did you kids have a good Christmas, and also a Happy New Year."

"Yes, Andy thanks to you and a Happy New year to you also."

"No problem and thank you."

"Jessie, stolen cars, need a name for a driver please."

"Craig Grant from Govan, sister lives in the village that is how he gets into the village."

"Come here Jessie, as he gave her a cuddle and a New Year's kiss."

"Haw big man when are we going to see you back here?"

"Six months maximum Jessie but I will be in for my tea as usual."

"Well, anything else you know where I am," she said laughing.

Andy went back to the car where Bobby was finishing off his cigarette.

"Bobby this car stinks."

"You can always walk back if you want, if not, stop moaning."

"What were you doing in there anyway?" continued Bobby.

"Wishing a friend, a good New Year."

"Oh, right no problem, straight to the office now Andy," said Bobby driving away from Bankvale.

"Hello this is Acting Detective Constable Andy Blackmore from Z Division headquarters," he said on the telephone.

"How are you doing mate, DC Barry Cruickshank here, what can I do for you.?"

"Do you know a guy named Craig Grant from your area.?"

"Craig Grant, car thief, scumbag, brilliant driver rarely gets caught in a chase, as you will know if you checked him out, he has convictions for car theft. A likeable scumbag" was the machinegun reply.

"Thank you I shall call you back if I get anything, Goodbye."

Andy sat and checked each of the reports and found the cars that had been recovered in and around the Govan area of Glasgow or near to there.

"DC Cruickshank? its Andy Blackmore again."

"Yeah." He muttered

"Do you have crime reports where stolen cars were found over here."

"Well after your last call I checked and we have six cars recovered in or around your neck of the woods in the past few weeks, why would that be.?"

"Because Grant has a sister over here."

"Oh, right never knew that and, call me Barry."

"Okay, Barry I shall submit intelligence report just now and get it sent over to you guys. with the update on him for future reference."

"Nice one mate thanks for that."

"Andy what are you up to mate," said Bobby.

"Doing the cars Bobby."

"Okay, how is it going?"

"Hopefully have someone locked up for it tomorrow."

"Yeah, sure thing mate" was the reply with a touch of "yeah right" about it.

"Good afternoon is that Fingerprints Department.?"

"Yes, it is."

"If I give you a car registration number and crime number can you check for a fingerprint match."

"I am sorry you have to submit a form with the suspects' name and details."

"oh, right I am sorry this is my first day as an AIDE nobody told me."

"Oh, bugger it, gimme the details," said the female receptionist.

Andy passed the details over the phone.

"How long do I have to wait for a reply please."

"How long is a piece of string mate?" was her reply.

"Oh Okay, thank you."

As the clock neared finishing time for Andy and Bobby, Andy began to pack everything into his allocated drawers to finish the shift when the phone on his desk rang. "ADC Blackmore, how can I help you?"

"You can't mate but I can help you, this is FPs here, we got you a hit on Craig Grant from the car."

"Magic, thank you so much."

"I will send you a statement in the internal mail," said the female caller.

Andy looked out the single crime report with the hit and filled in the suspects' details. He coded it accordingly.

"Bobby, what happens if the suspect for a crime lives outwith this area?"

"You contact the division and have him detained by them, after that you visit him."

"Okay, and if they say they are too busy.?"

"We have to wait."

"Don't like the sound of that at all" replied Andy.

"Andy what have you got."

"An FP hit on a stolen car."

"Already."

"Yep already" he replied rather pleased with himself.

"Good lad, time for home, the late shift is due in."

"Blackmore" came the shout from the DSs' room.

"Yes Sergeant,"

"You solved those crime reports yet," shouted DS Anderson from his room

"Almost, need tomorrow to get rid of a pile."

"Okay, you got tomorrow smart ass" came a further shout.

"Night Sergeant" as he passed the Sergeants office.

"Night Andy," was his reply without even looking up.

"Bobby, can you come in here a minute please, how did his first day go?"

"Stopped at a newsagent and he gets an FP hit on a stolen car can't ask for more than that"

"How the hell did he get that?"

"Haven't a bloody clue" replied Bobby "Does it matter he got a hit?"

"Thank you, close the door on your way out please" Bobby did as he was asked.

DS Anderson lifted his phone and dialled a number. "Hi, he is off to a flyer, just to let you know."

"Thank you" was the reply.

Back at the flat, an anxious Susan waited for Andy to find out how his first day went and what his colleagues were like. Over dinner, Andy filled Susan in on the events of the day for him. Susan enquired if she found out why he started on a Sunday rather than a Monday. Andy explained it was because of the public holidays and the way his shift pattern had fallen into that time. He was only working until Tuesday then off until Friday and then back into a full routine of shifts. Andy looked around and noticed that Susan had changed a few things around in the flat which they laughed about but he had to admit it did look better and less of a guy's pad.

"Back to work for you tomorrow then Susan" stated Andy.

"Yes, sure is, and living here I should be there in fifteen minutes and same coming home."

"That sounded nice," said Andy.

"What did.?"

"You saying coming home."

"Andy have you thought about how we are going to share the costs here," asked Susan.

"Actually, no I haven't but I could afford it on my own so should be no change."

"Well if we are going to save for a deposit for a house, we should think about it and get it sorted out."

"I have never been a spendthrift and I used to make loads when I was a brickie, so I have a little bit saved up for this day coming," said Andy.

"Me also but I never thought it would be for a house."

"Okay, how about we see what we need for the deposit and you can use yours if you want for the furnishings bit by bit as we go along."

"Yeah we could think about that also," said Susan.

The following morning, Andy and Susan set off at separate times for work as Andy started at eight o'clock with a morning briefing from DS Anderson. The briefing followed the same format as Andy got on his shift. Crime reports were allocated to the detectives except for Andy.

"Do you have any for me, Sergeant."

"No not this morning," he said walking away.

Bobby, Gordon, and Danny all looked at Andy who shrugged his shoulders as they looked at each other, nothing was said at that point.

Bobby suggested to Andy that after he made the tea, he should plan to have Craig Grant detained and he would go over with him to carry out the interview.

"That would be great thanks," said Andy.

DS Anderson entered the room and said that he had got a phone call and that Craig Grant had been arrested and charged with theft of motor cars in both divisions.

"Andy can you get in touch with DC Cruickshank and provide him with all the details of the cars from here as they are going to do the roll-up."

"Sergeant," said Bobby "That was Andy's information and his 'body' if you think about it, he should be the one doing this case."

"Aye well, they got him, and they are doing the case" as he left the office as if without a care in the world, "case solved" were his last words.

Bobby stood there shaking his head, Danny and Gordon came over to Andy to lift their cups of tea.

"Sorry about that big man," said Danny "that is absolute crap he was yours" he continued

"Ten crimes solved I suppose, what hurts more is I am probably off the New Years' honours list now and not getting my visit to the Palace" commented Andy. They all burst out laughing.

Andy did as requested and called DC Cruickshank and passed on the information he required. After the business side of things were done, he asked why his division had gone to get Grant. Barry Cruickshank said quietly they were under orders from their Detective Superintendent to go get him, "Andy, Detective Super' getting involved in a few stolen cars virtually unheard-of mate"

"Listen, no problem" replied Andy.

"If it is any consolation, he was your capture and we all know that over here, good luck with your secondment."

"Thanks," said Andy as he hung up the receiver.

"Well?" Said Bobby as Gordon and Danny looked over.

"Some Detective Super' gave the order to go and get Grant."

They looked at Andy with incredulity, "A Detective Superintendent? Involved with stolen cars? You are having a laugh?" asked Gordon

"Well that is what has come from over the river" replied Andy "See at the end of the day, saves me a pile of writing, but we all know who got the body for this one, so, if you guys need me to solve anything and you do the writing let me know," he said laughing heading for the office door.

Andy left the room and went to the toilet and when he got back Gordon asked Andy to accompany him on an enquiry.

"Where are you two going," said the DS as they passed his open door.

"I have an enquiry and I thought it would be good for Andy to get out and about and meet a few people in this area as he knows most of the neds in his place," said Gordon

"Yeah, why not, but I need him back here sharpish, there is a load of filing to be done" which brought a glance of surprise from Yardley.

Andy and Gordon drove up to spill hill where they went and interviewed a potential witness to a few housebreakings that had been happening in the area.

"You're Andy Blackmore, aren't you?" Said the man who was unknown to Andy.

"Archie Devine" as he held out his hand to shake Andy's "Nice to meet you at last."

"How do you know me we have never met.?"

"We have mutual friends and the word on the street is you are a fair man unlike some, are you in the CID now Andy.?"

"Yes and no it's just a six-month secondment."

"Well don't let that six months change you then," said Devine.

"Right, Andy I have everything we need" after about an hour or so.

"Nice to meet you, Mr Devine," said Andy as he stood up to leave the house

"Call me Archie."

"Okay, Archie" he replied looking at Devine

Gordon had interviewed Archie Devine and he revealed some interesting information about the housebreakings in the area.

"Big man, I know you work in this area, how the hell does Devine know you?" asked Gordon when they returned to their vehicle.

"Gordon, honestly man, not got a clue, what he did say was we have a mutual friend, now that concerns me, not greatly, but everywhere I go people seem to know who I am, well, know my name."

"Well, as Bobby said this is going to be interesting with you around."

"Fancy some fun, Gordon."

"Now that makes me nervous" he replied.

"Drive through Bankvale please, slowly," requested Andy

The CID car was driven through Bankvale Andy spotted an old friend walking along the road. "Gordon pull over," he asked, then alighting from the car as it stopped.

"Come on Gordon," said Andy.

Gordon got out of the car but watching all around him knowing what this area could be like.

"Hughie my man," said Andy extending a hand of friendship to the local worthy in his late sixties.

"Andy" was his one-word reply eyeing him with suspicion at the greeting.

"Right Hughie here is the deal with no options, I am seconding you as my deputy sheriff down here, so no housebreakings, that means the houses and the shops, and the word is the poachers get a free run on the river, within reason, now I can't do anything about the river bailiffs," said Andy.

Gordon stood looking at Andy in disbelief.

"Well, Hughie.?"

Hughie stood looking around himself. Hughie was a wise old man; he was the man the village looked up to in times of disputes on the river.

"Do I have an option?" asked Hughie.

"Yes absolutely" replied Andy as Hughie looked at him weighing up his options without a word being exchanged.

Hughie held out his right hand, "deal" he said, "deal" replied Andy shaking Hughie's hand.

"I don't believe you two," said Gordon a witness to what had just happened.

"No', be that when you get salmon for breakfast" replied Hughie.

As they were going back to the office Andy asked what Devine meant and being in the CID and it changing him. Gordon assured him that he had nothing to worry about. When they got into the car park at the office Gordon turned to Andy "Listen, kid," he said "Grant was yours, something not right so I and the boys have had a chat"

"And.?"

"We all share and should share information we get, so keep this in our office until we find out what is going on, we think something is not right at the moment, so this deal you got with Hughie you be careful, very careful."

"Gordon, I bet as long as I am here, we get nothing to investigate in the village as far as housebreaking go."

"Let's wait and see," replied Gordon.

"Okay," was Andy's reply.

"As they passed by the Sergeants door going back into their office the call came out, "Andy take these please and get them filed before you finish."

"Yes, no problem" he replied.

Andy returned with a pile of crime reports which he put on his desk and from a grey metal cabinet took out the relevant box files marked 1981.

Andy spent an hour of his day filing away the reports but two stood out which were reports of further fires. Andy added those to his other four that he had for enquiry.

Bobby passed Andy's desk and threw a bit of paper on the desk, one word, "Toilet." Andy lifted it as he followed Bobby into the gents then flushed it down the pan.

"Andy the DS is never like this with new starts, what is going on or whose cage have you rattled?"

"I haven't a clue, but it is early days I have not had a chance to rattle anyone's cage yet."

"Well something is going on and if continues then we shall have a word with him."

"Thanks, Bobby."

They both returned to the office to find DS Anderson standing there.

"Have you finished the filing yet?"

"Just about, considering the amount of them."

"Fine thanks what about your enquiries?"

"Well, the cars are all wrapped up just the multiple vandalisms and the fires to sort out."

"See what you can do with them, experienced detectives have tried the fires and got nothing so I don't think you will either so don't waste much time on them."

"I have a job for you in the morning, no suit, casual clothing, have you got that?" asked DS Anderson.

"Yes."

"Bobby that goes for you also."

"Sure, thing Sergeant" was his reply looking at him with some suspicion.

Andy and Bobby just looked at each other in silence and with a shrug of their shoulders.

Andy finished off the filing and turned to the crime reports relating to the wilful fire-raisings. He went over each one with a fine-tooth comb. There was a person of interest who was a local businessman and well respected in the area. He lived in a very smart part of the town and was married with a family. His wife worked in a local bonded warehouse, but nobody knew why as they appeared well off. She had been in the bottling plant since she left school and Andy's thoughts were "good for her to keep working maybe that is where all her friends were also."

This one he wanted to solve and this time he was going to keep his mouth shut if he found anything even from his colleagues. Lesson learned from the stolen cars' enquiry. Andy placed all the fire-raising crime reports into his desk drawer before making his way home.

"Hiya, how was your first day back at school? as he wrapped his arms around Susan

"Well the engagement ring was a sensation in the staff room and classroom but not unexpected by some of them, the kids were themselves."

"How was your day.?"

"Looks like someone is interfering again as a case I had information on, was stolen by another Divisions CID then I got dumped with a load of filing to do for the DS. The boys said something is going on as the DS never treats the new starts the way he is having a go at me."

"Andy are you not getting a little paranoid about outside influences interfering.?"

"Maybe I am, maybe I am not, all will come out in the wash soon enough."

"Just watch what you are doing please" she paused "Anyway dinner is ready."

"Susan I need to go out for an hour to the pub I know someone there that can help me with an enquiry I have been given, I just need some background information and what to look for that others may have missed during the original enquiries, you can come if you wish"

"No thanks I have a little homework to do for school tomorrow."

Andy made his way down to the pub after dinner on his own, his target was an old friend Chris Banks who had risen through the ranks of the Fire Service to become a Commander. Chris was a regular in the pub and well respected. Andy had met him through mutual friends when he arrived in the area. Andy sat facing the door watching for Chris who entered the bar at exactly eight o'clock, the joke was if your watch had stopped wait for Chris getting into the pub on time. Chris went straight to the bar, "half and a half-pint please" there was no need for him to ask as all the bar staff knew his order, it never changed for one day to the next.

"Hi Andy, how is the job going, I hear you have been moved to the CID."

"Yes, it is just a secondment, six months max."

"I know you are in your own time here Chris, but could I have a word with you please?"

"Sure."

"I have been given an enquiry relating to wilful fire-raisings."

"Okay."

"The value of the property damaged is well over a million pounds and nobody has been arrested the general view of the bosses and some of the cops is that all the fires have been insurance jobs."

"Your feeling is what Andy?" asked Chris as he took a sip of lager.

"Too many, too soon in the same area, something is missing in the enquiry, but my problem is I am new to the department and don't want to rock the boat, I was told experienced detectives found nothing and I have not much hope either if any."

"What do you have just now.?"

"Only time, location and cause."

"Which is.?"

"All after ten o'clock at night but before midnight, locations, shop and industrial factories, cause, the likelihood of petrol as an accelerant."

"What are your thoughts, Chris?"

"My thoughts are, taking what you have told me at face value I would say you have a wilful

fire-raiser these are not insurance jobs, but the work of someone acting on his or her own for some reason" he replied.

"So, what am I looking for.?"

"Could be someone who has a grudge against the business owner or company, could be someone who just enjoys lighting fires and watching the flames, could be someone who loves fire engines, sirens, blue lights watching the firemen trying to control the blaze.

"The last part is, is there a possibility that the person who started the fire could still be around when the Fire Brigade arrives at the locus and maybe even when the police were there.?"

"Yes, I believe that person could be there or very close by, what you have Andy is either a criminal or a pyromaniac or maybe even both the person may even have personal problems from the past or even the present it is quite a deep subject."

"Chris this has given me a head start thank you," said Andy.

"Hey what is this about you being engaged?" asked Chris.

"Yes, it is true."

"Congratulations to you and Susan."

"Thanks, Chris, I shall let you know how this goes."

As he left the pub passing the bar, he ordered a half and a half pint for Chris.

"One in the tap for you Chris and thanks again."

Andy returned to the flat and Susan was beavering away at the table, papers everywhere.

"How was your meeting?" she asked

"Very interesting."

"Oh, dad was on the phone looking for you."

"Why.?"

"I don't know, call him back please."

"Hello Brian, were you looking for me? Susan said you were."

"Yes, just to let you know I spoke to Ricky and sorted things out."

"Thank you for that, one down two to go, bye for now."

"What was that all about," said Susan.

"Just part of the clearing the air discussion."

"Okay," said Susan giving Andy a look of suspicion.

"Think I shall head for a shower what about you."

"I can't all these papers will get wet."

"Geez, you are bad as your mother."

"Meaning what exactly?" she asked drawing him a look of curiosity.

"You are your mothers' daughter, great sense of humour."

Susan stood up and kissed Andy, "Go get your shower big boy," she said playfully.

"See what I mean," he said laughing.

"Where are you going dressed like that?" asked Susan the following morning when she saw Andy ready for work.

"Honestly, I don't know, just told to turn up like this."

"See you tonight love you," said Andy giving Susan a parting kiss on her cheek.

DS Anderson gave the morning briefing, followed by "You two go see the Divisional Commander" looking at Bobby and Andy.

"Can I ask, why him?" asked Bobby.

"Don't know, he would not say to anyone" replied Anderson.

Andy and Bobby made their way down the corridor to be faced with a closed, light oak door with a bronze plate on the door with "Divisional Commander" inscribed on it. Bobby knocked on the door "Enter" came the shout from within.

"Good morning Sir," Bobby and Andy said almost in unison.

"Good morning gentlemen sit down please."

The Divisional Commander generally referred to as the Div Com. sat silently. He was scanning some papers. He leaned over the desk handing both a brown file.

"You may open it he said" leaning back into his chair and clasping his hands resting them on his stomach.

Bobby and Andy sat and read the short report which had been prepared for them. They both closed the files within seconds of each other and handed them back to the boss.

"Any questions.?"

"Yes, sir I have," said Andy.

"Go ahead."

"Why me, I have hardly had time to warm the seat I occupy. What do I know about this?"

"Okay, why you? You have a reputation for information gathering and you can handle yourself, now your methods are rather dubious, to say the least, but we all know you can, also you are not connected."

"What does that mean sir?" asked Andy.

"You know exactly what it means" was his short sharp reply catapulting himself towards his desk from his relaxed laid-back position

"Why me also sir?" asked Bobby.

"Because you are a top-class detective and you can keep this cowboy on a short leash, also you are not connected" he continued.

"Nobody other than me within this office knows about this. You report directly to me nobody else."

"Who knows out-with this job, sir?"

"A few from an outside agency, both go home and report back here at seven o'clock tonight, I will meet you here."

"What about our shift today sir.?"

"I shall deal with that."

"How long do we stay on this sir?" Asked Bobby.

"Until the job is done" was the reply ending the conversation.

Andy and Bobby went back to their room and they were immediately questioned by Danny and Gordon. DS Anderson walked in "What's going on Andy?"

Bobby immediately interjected. "The Divisional Commander will speak to you Sergeant; we are going home now" as they left the office leaving everyone confused about their sudden departure.

Chapter Three

❚❚ Oh, you are home early Andy," said Susan as she got into the flat, "Is everything okay?"

"Yes, there has been a change of plan for this week at work I am starting at seven tonight."

"Why?"

"Susan I cannot discuss this with anyone honestly."

"I had this with dad, so I understand" she replied.

"Thank you."

At six-thirty that evening Andy left the house for the second time that day to go to the office. At seven o'clock he and Bobby were in the Divisional Commanders office. The remit was to observe and report back personally to him each morning. Their written report had to be in a sealed envelope which had not to be left anywhere or with anyone. Under no circumstances had there to be copies kept by anyone they were warned.

"Okay, guys part two of the remit read and digest" was his order handing them more papers.

Andy and Bobby read the reports,

Jeanna Roberts, age 14, a pupil of St Angelo RC School, Bankvale, tall, slim, blond.

Angelina Blake, age 13 pupil of St Angelo RC School, Bankvale, tall, slim, black hair.

Both girls attended the said school and were taken into care following allegations that they were being subjected to sex parties involving local businessmen, dignitaries, and others. Initial enquiries by Social Workers revealed that they were attending those parties, but both denied any sexual involvement.

Large amounts of cash were found in their rooms by their parents who informed the Social Workers of their concerns as neither could justify having such large amounts. Emergency placements were found in a local children's home.

"Now you both know the details are you guys okay with this?"

"Yes sir," said Andy.

"Yes sir," said Bobby.

"Good that is the answer I was hoping for" he paused.

"Don't burst my budget maximum of twelve hours a shift."

"Yes, sir."

"There is a car in the garage for you, unmarked, no aerial visible when you finish, leave it somewhere out on the street or in a street near your home whoever is driving, pick each other up before each shift away from here, as for getting the report to me I will meet you at the council dump each morning at seven, see you in the morning."

10 pm: Sitting along from the children's home watching everyone that moved in the area, a red Ford Escort pulled up outside. From their position, they saw two people climb out a ground floor bedroom window and get into the car which made off.

"Okay, here we go as they set off at a safe distance behind. They travelled to the north side of the city where the car came to a halt in among the red tenement buildings. The driver got out and opened the rear door of the vehicle and under the streetlights, they identified two females alighting from the rear of the vehicle. The descriptions matched that of Jeanna and Angelina. All three went into the close. Andy and Bobby watched as a light went on in the front room of the top floor flat. They then saw a blonde female looking out the window overlooking the street.

From eleven at night to five in the morning every hour on the hour a car arrived sometime a lone occupant sometimes several occupants all going into the same close. Andy and Bobby noted the make and registration number of each car and the number of occupants. Each car left forty-five minutes exactly after arrival. About five-fifteen the following morning the Ford Escort left with the two girls. Andy and Bobby watched as they climbed into the home via the back-bedroom window under the cover of the winter darkness.

7 am: The sealed envelope was handed to the boss through the open window of his car.

"Same time tomorrow lads please," as he drove off watched by his two officers.

Bobby just looked at Andy then said "I will drop you off at your flat and then tonight pick you up at the bus stop opposite your place"

"Thank you that would be great" replied Andy.

"Good morning Susan," as he handed her tea and toast in bed with a kiss.

"Good morning love of my life how was your night," she asked.

"long night to be honest and I need my bed, I shall wait until you get up or maybe you won't get to school."

"Make sure you are still in here when I get home then."

"See you later," said Susan as she left for school.

"Hey, you," said Susan shaking Andy to waken him.

"Eh?" was his drowsy reply rubbing his eyes.

"It is four-thirty."

"Susan.?"

"Oh, were you expecting someone else.?"

"Mmmmm duvet time, Oh I think this is a lovely way to finish the working day."

Showered and changed as Susan made dinner Andy was ready for his shift.

"Did all go well last night?" asked Susan

"Yes" was the one-word reply.

"How was your day?"

"Pretty good but I got a new kid in the class that was expelled from another school for being violent and disruptive."

"Are you guys trained in confrontation reduction or self-defence even just a little?"

"Of course not, we are teachers."

"Right gym for you even the basics can help."

"Dinner was lovely thank you," he said rising from the table.

"See you in the morning," said Andy kissing her forehead and cuddling her.

At the arranged time Bobby picked up Andy. Bobby and Andy set up the "watch" on the home from a distance. At nine-thirty that night a blue Ford Cortina arrived and parked where the Escort had parked. This time there was no other movement from the home. This now proved to be a waiting game.

10:30 pm: Two girls ran down the grass embankment from the home, One was identified as Jeanna the other was not Angelina but someone smaller and heavier. Bobby and Andy looked at each other wondering what was going on and how many of these kids in there were involved in whatever was going on. Before the one who was possibly Jeanna got into the car they saw the driver of the car strike her across the face and throw her into the car.

The Cortina made off at a speed which surprised Bobby and Andy initially and they caught up as the car headed towards the motorway and not towards the north side of the city. A short time later they exited the motorway and headed into one of the most highly sought-after areas on the outskirts of the city. Bobby pulled back as the car slowed down and stopped outside the controlled gates of a massive villa set deep back off the road the lights barely visible at the top of a winding tree-lined road.

Parking was not going to be easy as there were no cars parked on the roadway to conceal them. This was an area that housed the crème de la crème of the city, the rich and the famous. Andy walked past the house as Bobby parked up at the nearby T Junction among other cars. They were in luck the houses formed a cul de sac, so only one way in and out, "Bingo" thought Bobby. Andy returned to the car, "nothing no name on the wall or the gates, just number six on the letterbox".

Andy glanced at his watch as the first car arrived at eleven o'clock the same as last night. Large, black, top of the range Mercedes, slowed down at the gates and turned left up the private road.

The same format as the night before continued the hour every hour until four in the morning, top of the range cars coming and going carrying single, double, and triple occupants. At five o'clock the car carrying the girls left the road and headed back towards the home. Bobby and Andy watched as the girls climbed back in through the back window as they did the night before.

7 am: Once more the sealed envelope was handed over "thanks, guys."

"Boss we need another car."

"Okay, pick it up tonight from the council car park someone will meet you with the keys."

Andy was taken home by Bobby.

"Mmmmmmm Mr Blackmore good morning indeed," said Susan
"Oh, have I wakened you, Miss Berger?"

"This is better than tea and toast trust me" as they snuggled under the duvet.

"Andy, I am away; see you later love you" Susan shouted rushing out of the door.

"Love you also" he replied before turning over to sleep.

Andy's alarm went off at five o'clock for a seven o'clock start. He got up and looked around the flat, no sign of Susan. He had a shower and as he wrapped himself in a towel there was a knock at the door. Looking through the viewer he saw June and Joe.

"Hey guys come in please let me get something on."

"Andy came back into the living room, what do I owe the pleasure of this visit guys great to see you."

"Andy," said June, "have you heard the news today."

"No, I just got up a short time ago I have been doing constant nights."

"Andy there is an ongoing incident at the school the place is in lockdown."

"Okay," he replied.

"The block where the incident is, we think is where Susan maybe as she has not come out yet."

"Okay, I know that she is the deputy headteacher but since she went back, she is teaching again non-stop as somebody is off ill, she also said that in her class there was a kid expelled from another school for being violent and disruptive."

"It was the Divisional Commander that contacted our office and spoke to the Sergeant. "Now we don't know what you are involved in, but his message was to suspend the operation until school situation resolved" and it is the same message going to Bobby. Do you know what he means."?

"Yes, thank you," replied Andy

"Am I allowed to go down to the school.?"

"Andy we are sorry but the answer to that is no."

"Are you guys here to babysit me by chance.?" he asked.

"Well not exactly," said June.

"June?" Andy said as if quizzing her in a raised voice.

June explained that they were instructed by the boss to make sure he did not go near the school as the last thing they needed was him going in there "all guns blazing" and creating a situation the force could not justify or protect him from. They were also worried that any intrusion could endanger the lives of any teacher or pupil in there. Senior officers were aware of Andy's unorthodox methods of dealing with things, but this was one they could not take a chance with publicly.

"Okay," said Andy "can we go to the school as in the three of us and I promise I will stay with you guys at all times in the car or wherever." Just at that, the telephone rang.

"Hello."

"Andy it is Brian."

"Okay,"

"We are watching the news what is going on down there at Susan's school is she home.?"

"No Brian she is not home."

"Is she in there in the school.?"

"I don't know I don't have the news on."

"I thought you were day shift."

"Well Brian things in life are never what they seem are they.?"

"Don't you get smart-arsed with me."

"Remember Brian I can do what I like with you remember.?"

"Andy it is Sandra what have you said to him he is raging."

"Sandra this is no time for arguing, Susan is not here, I have not seen the news, so I don't know what is happening right now. I will call you when I can and update you."

"Thank you, Andy."

June and Joe could hear everything that was being said between Brian and Andy. They sat there trying not to feel awkward.

"Well guys who need a retired senior cop as a father in law in the future, not me that is for sure, right back to us."

"Can I phone the boss?" said June.

June put Andy's proposal to their Sergeant. She listened intently to his reply as Andy made tea.

"Right big man here is the script," said June. "The Sergeant is highly dubious about your motives of wanting to go near the school at this time other than to be near Susan. He understands your need to be there. So, what he is proposing is that Joe and I take you down there in our car, you have not to use your own. Also, we have sole responsibility for you and if you do anything silly, we are going to be held responsible and you are going back to the building sites, your call Andy."

"I agree, I just need to be there when Susan gets out of there, I promise you both no madness."

"Okay, let's go then."

Joe parked the police vehicle on the street just inside the police cordon. Andy asked what was happening and Joe said that a police negotiator was speaking to the person holding the teachers and pupils the last time he heard. Andy wanted to know everything they knew, and Joe told him that this had been ongoing since one o'clock that afternoon. Early shift and back shift had doubled up and that the school was surrounded by officers. They were surprised that he was not around as they knew he was day shift.

"Andy," said June.

"How was your Christmas and New Year."

"Is that a loaded question June you are hopeless at asking questions with that tone" he laughed.

"Okay, we were watching the drama unfold about your brother is he alright now."

"Yes, he is thank you, well as good as can be expected given the circumstances the truth is between us that he has damaged parts of his brain he may never be the same again."

"What does he do for a living Andy.?"

"Oh, he is the brains of the family he is a chemist."

"Will this affect his work."

"Probably."

"That's a shame."

"What about you guys."

"We had a great time with the kids, to be honest," said Joe.

June was rather quiet on the subject "June what about you.?"

"Yeah, it was fine."

"June.?"

"I said it was fine Andy just another day to me."

June pulled down the passenger seat visor and opened the mirror pretending to fix her eyebrow but staring at Andy sitting in the back seat. Andy saw her gaze and nodded. June replaced the visor upright. Andy knew something was amiss with June.

"Well your father in law is not your best pal by the sound of it Andy what about Sandra," said June.

"Well for a start they are not the in-laws yet June so that is a bonus, as for Sandra she is lovely."

"Was she a lecturer at the City university in years gone by.?"

"I think she was a teacher somewhere" replied Andy.

"Do you remember my friend Sheena from the Christmas night out Andy she knows her well."

"Ah right Okay."

A short time later, an Armed Response Vehicle, known as an ARV, raced through the open gates into the school playground and out of public view.

"Is that them just getting here for god's sake?" said Andy.

"Everything takes time mate.," said Joe.

Joe looked in the rear-view mirror and saw Andy was getting restless with the apparent lack of progress and silence on the radios. Joe then saw Andy taking something from his jacket pocket and hang it around his neck, It was his warrant card.

"Andy chill mate you promised us."

"Yes, I know."

"Would you mind if I stretched my legs outside.?"

"Can I come with you.?" asked June.

"Yes, certainly I made you guys a promise I shall not break it."

Andy got out the car with June directly behind him as he walked over to a stone wall. Leaning back, arms folded with one foot resting the wall he stood staring at the school.

"Okay, June talk to me," he said as she stood next to him.

"What about?" she asked.

"You and Sheena."

"There is no me and Sheena."

"Explain please," he said looking at her.

"Sheena is Sheena a free spirit I am more a loyal and true type."

"She was seeing someone over the Christmas New Year period when I was working"

"Do you know who."

"Yes, and so do you."

"So, I have decided my time with her is over and I am going back to the male species."

"Oh, June does that mean I am back in with a shout then," he said trying to make light of the situation.

"Andy you are always in with a shout and you only just started with the CID, but I miss you."

"Haw Andy" came a shout from the gathering crowd "Get yersel down there big man and sort out whoever is in there with our kids."

"Hey Andy, is your girlfriend still in there? shouted another" that one shocked him, as he did not know that the locals knew about his relationship with Susan.

He walked over to the locals who were behind metal barriers and spoke to them.

"Guys this is one of my best mates in the job this is June most of you know her. I made her a promise I would not interfere in this situation" as someone else shouted over to him about Susan, "yes, my girlfriend is in there with your kids so really, we are all in this together so right now my nerves are jangling like yours."

"Andy, tell your mates if this is not over soon, we are going to sort it out ourselves"

"Barry, if anyone here makes a stupid move like that it could cost kids and teachers their lives."

"Aye, you ya prick listen to the big man," said a local worthy full of the drink.

"Tell you what guys since I got here you have all been good to me so if I hear anything, I will let you know what is happening."

"Thanks, Andy a few shouted."

Andy went back and sat in the car with June.

Radio and television broadcasters were rolling up with their outside broadcasting units at the ready. Locals were being interviewed for the late-night news to be circulated throughout the UK.

Andy was thinking of the kids that he should be watching over tonight with Bobby but at the end of the day Susan was is the number one priority.

Just before midnight, the radios wakened up as messages began to be transmitted. To all late shift personnel return to the office, one male in custody being taken to Headquarters by the ARV team.

News spread quickly that the situation had been resolved peacefully as an orderly stream of parents made their way down towards the school. It was a surreal line of silent parents going to collect their children under the streetlights.

Andy thanked June and Joe as he got out of the vehicle and he joined the line of parents. The blue lights from attending ambulances who were on standby bounced off the building and playground. The Fire Brigade got the stand down from their control room and retreated to their stations.

As Andy entered the school by the main door the headteacher and his deputy headteacher stood to direct parents towards the school gymnasium to collect their children.

"Hey, how was your day at school?" Andy asked

"Eventful to say the least," replied Susan with a smile

They just stood there wrapped in each other's arms refusing to let go as the tears flooded from Susan like a massive water fountain. They were tears of relief that everything had ended without the loss of life or injury. Parents took their children home hand in hand, arm in arm, some of the mothers in tears like Susan.

"Andy Blackmore is that tears in your eyes," said Susan.

"Yeah, tears of joy you are alright."

"Haw big man your girlfriend alright then."

"Yeah she is good thanks," he said to the enquirer.

"Well, see as long as she is here, she will always be alright.

The headteacher gathered his staff together he announced that the school would be closed later that day and asked everyone to return the following day.

Andy and Susan returned to her car the doors were being locked and the lights extinguished in the classrooms by the janitor plunging the playground into darkness.

"Will you drive please?" asked a tearful Susan.

"Yes of course."

"Why are you not at work Andy.?"

"I don't believe you asked that, home time."

They got into the flat and the answering machine on the phone was showing twelve missed calls and messages from the Berger and Blackmore households plus a few friends.

"You better phone home Susan."

"Andy this is home now I will phone mum and dad."

"Mum I am okay," said Susan having called her parents.

"Yes, I am going to bed I need sleep."

"Yes, Andy is here I will call you tomorrow."

"Goodnight."

"Alice, Ricky it is Andy just to let you know everything is alright with Susan sorry to call so late" was the message left on their answering machine

Susan came back into the living room. "Can I have a large Brandy please."

"Sure, then bed."

Two large brandies were slowly consumed in almost silence. Andy was waiting for Susan to speak; Susan was reflecting on what she and her colleagues and pupils had gone through that day and grateful that everyone had got out alive. Andy looked at the clock as he turned out the lights it was almost three in the morning. For Susan it was to be a day off, for Andy he would back on his special mission with Bobby for another twelve hours shift.

Chapter Four

S usan spent most of the day on the phone to her parents and friends and the phone never seemed to stop with callers wishing her well. Andy decided to get her out of the flat and let the answering machine take the strain for a while, so they decided on a late lunch come early dinner at their local pub.

A young waitress approached their table with her notepad in hand ready to take their order,

"Oh, hello Miss Berger."

"Oh hello, Kerry are you working here now.?"

"Yes, Miss."

"Okay, Kerry you have left school now and eighteen so from today I am Susan, and this is my fiancée, Andy."

"Pleased to meet you, Kerry," said Andy.

"Nice to meet you also Sir" she replied.

"Do you mean Andy?" he said laughing.

"Yes, that's what I meant," as she looked into his blue eyes blushing.

"We shall keep this simple, two prawn cocktails for starters, two scampi main courses with chips."

"Great and anything to drink?"

"Glass of white wine for me," said Susan.

"Fresh orange juice for me please I am driving," said Andy.

Susan told Andy that she was so proud of Kerry as she completed her sixth-year studies and got straight "A"s in several subjects including English, Maths, Biology and Music plus two other subjects she did just for fun. What made her special was she had a very tough start in life and was brought up for years in the local children's home, but she proved that no matter where you are brought up you can do well.

"Andy are you listening to me?" said Susan.

"Yes, she seems a very bright young lady."

"There you go, folks, two prawn cocktails, enjoy please," said Kerry as she walked away

"Thank you," they said.

"When did she leave the home and where is she living now.?"

"I don't know I shall ask her."

Another waitress took away the empty glasses that held the prawn cocktail just minutes before Kerry delivered the main course.

"Scampi and Chips managed to get you a few extra chips," said Kerry laughing.

"Good girl," said Andy.

"Oh, I think you have a new admirer Andy B."

"Behave you."

Dinner finished they relaxed in the lounge freeing up the table for other diners. Kerry walked over and being assured they were finished she brought the bill which Andy paid in cash.

"I heard what happened at the school yesterday I am glad you are alright."

"Thank you."

"Do you know something Susan, seems strange calling you Susan, but you were my inspiration at school, and I could not have had a better mentor. You were like a mum and dad all in one to me."

"So, what comes next Kerry.?"

"University, I have been accepted to three, but I think I shall accept St Andrews to get away from this hellhole and the bad memories it holds."

"Do you have a place to live, Kerry?"

"Yes, the Social Work Department and the Housing Department got me sorted out, I will be forever grateful to my Social Worker for the rest of my life."

"How long have you been living in supported accommodation?" asked Susan.

"Six months now."

"Changing the subject Miss, I mean Susan where can I get one of those please" looking at Andy.

"Well you don't Kerry they broke the mould after making him, so he is a one-off"

"Damn Okay," she said laughing as she went back to her work.

"Told you, new admirer."

"Interesting."

"What does that mean?" asked Susan.

"Nothing," said Andy as he watched the staff looking over.

As they were leaving Andy beckoned for Kerry to come to him and Susan, he slipped five pounds into her hand, "your tip for service with a smile Kerry"

"I can't take that"

"Yes, you can university is expensive, you go on and be someone's inspiration." Said Susan as she left the premises smiling towards Kerry.

7 pm: Andy met up with Bobby away from the office and made their way to the council car park. There they met someone who handed them a set of car keys twenty-four hours later than planned as arranged by the boss.

"How is your girlfriend Andy," asked Bobby.

"At the moment she is good, but I don't know what will happen when she goes back tomorrow."

"At least she got out alive and I am happy for you both."

"Thanks, Bobby."

They headed down to the road alongside the home. Engine off seats rolled back they began to relax as nothing was going to happen for a while as they were early.

"Do you think we missed anything last night Bobby?"

"Probably"

"Okay, let's think, we have been North, and we have been South are we working our way around the compass, if we go East or West tonight, we missed the opposite last night"

"Geezuz Andy, what is next from you Newtons Theory of Relativity?"

"No Bobby that is tomorrow night once I know what it is" As they started having a laugh about that one a black, top of the range Jeep appeared, neither paid much attention to it until they saw the back window open and Jeanna and Angelina bail out of it straight to the jeep containing the driver and passenger.

"Christ game on early tonight," remarked Bobby

They followed the vehicle into the west end of the city, slowly through the busy main thoroughfare heaving with traffic. They watched as the vehicle indicated left searching for a parking space, but eventually double parking holding up traffic behind them. The front-seat passenger got out followed by the girls. This was not part of the plan as Andy got out also.

"Andy" shouted Bobby

"Go park then find me"

Andy followed for a short distance and watched as the trio went into the Valentino club used by the local gentry and those that could afford to live in the west end of the city. Directly opposite the club was a coffee bar with a full-size window, top to bottom, side to side, with an unobstructed view of the entrance. A timber shelf stretched from end to end with single stools equally spaced out. Menus with numerous types of coffees and cakes were on display on the shelf.

"Can I get you something sir?" asked the waitress.

"Eh, large black coffee please."

"Coming right up sir."

The coffee was placed in front of him as he observed the comings and goings at the club" "Em your coffee sir" said the waitress.

"Oh, thank you" replied Andy wrapping the window with his knuckles as Bobby wandered past looking for him. Bobby entered the premises via the large glass door and sat beside Andy.

"Andy this is Mission Impossible tonight."

"Bobby, nothing is impossible, it just takes a little longer."

"Coffee sir?"

"Can I have a black coffee, no milk please" replied Bobby.

"Certainly."

"Your coffee and your bill are on the tab."

"West End prices is it?" asked Andy.

"Of course, sir," said the waitress smiling.

"Where did you get parked.?"

"Pure luck big man just down the road clear view of the footpath outside the club."

"Bobby, we have a problem here that this could be a walk-up venue, train, subway, car, taxi."

"Andy, I get nervous when you think."

"Oh, then you don't want to know what I know about the crime reports I have for the fires then."

"Look," said Andy as he looked to the upper floor of the club

"What? Where?"

"The light in the upper part of the club has been lit."

"There is Angelina at the window," said Andy.

"Bobby this is not good sitting here."

"What do you mean?"

"Okay, mate your call as the boss, car or club?"

"Car for me," said Bobby

"Club for me then" replied Andy.

"Andy no."

"Andy yes" he replied getting up from his stool and striding out of the coffee shop, crossing the road and straight into the club having been stopped and searched by a bouncer on the way in.

"Sir your friend did not pay the bill," said the waitress which she presented to Bobby.

"Okay, love, here you go, keep the change" handing her a few pounds.

Bobby went back to the car and embedded himself in the passengers' seat as if to wait for the driver if anyone peered into the vehicle.

"Pint of heavy please," said Andy to the barman. Andy watched as the pint was poured then laid on the bar. He handed the barman a ten-pound note and received his change. He looked around the bar and saw a set of stairs going to an upper floor. The bar was busy considering it was early.

"Hey," said Andy to the barman, "are there any seats upstairs?"

"Sorry mate, that is for club members only."

"Oh, alright sorry never been in here before."

"No problem mate lots ask that question."

"Busy night for you?" asked Andy.

"Yeah, but it will get busier just the time of the year" he replied.

"Do you own the place?" inquired Andy.

"Hell, I wish, listen you look a big guy, we are looking for a bouncer here can you handle yourself?"

"Not my thing to be honest."

"Oh well if you change your mind come see me, I am the chargehand."

"Big man, what's your name?"

"Andy, Andy White."

"And you are?"

"Willie Boyle" replied the barman.

Andy finished his pint and made to leave but he went back to the bar and shook Willie's hand "nice to meet you maybe I shall give your offer some thought but I chucked all that bouncer stuff after years of doing it in Ibiza and Majorca"

"the club, is it private or do you just have to be a local?"

"It is a private smokers club,"

"Oh, Willie like a gentleman's club, then smoker's night, I don't smoke so no use to me"

Willie laughed out loud "No problem big man"

"See ya Willie love this place good old-fashioned pub"

As Andy went out onto the street, he stood with his hands in the pockets of his leather jacket and took in a deep breath of fresh air. He had a fair idea where his car was parked as he turned left to see Brian Berger and DS Anderson coming up the road towards him. "Oh, shit not them he thought" as he ran across the road to the coffee shop going inside." He watched them enter 'Valentinos'.

"Hi again said the waitress your friend paid the bill."

"Do you know I felt so bad about that I wanted to check he had enough money."

"Yes, he did thank you for returning," she said looking at him.

"You are welcome."

Andy's heart was pounding by this time, "think Andy think" was going through his head, he stepped out again onto the street and was confronted by Bobby who had seen him running across the road.

"You gonna tell me what is going on Andy."

"Yes, I promise, gimme five minutes and you stay out of this please."

"Why?"

"Because I am asking Bobby, please."

"Sure."

Andy went back over to the club, "you back big man" said the bouncer."

"Yeah, Willie spoke to me about a vacancy here."

"Oh, right you look the type we need here."

"I will be out in a minute."

Andy went in and did a quick 360-degree scan of the place no sign of Berger or Anderson anywhere. Andy went back outside and spoke to the bouncer.

"See the two guys that went in a minute ago I am sure one is an old mate from the past, but I can't see him in there."

"Probably upstairs mate."

"Upstairs?"

"Trust me you don't want to know if you get a start, tips are great, the mouth is shut tight."

"Right, thanks, I need money just now and lots of it."

"Well, this is the door for you" replied the burly bouncer.

"Thanks."

Andy went down the road away from the club, crossing over out of sight of the bouncer who had lost interest in him anyway. He got into the car beside Bobby.

"Right you gonna tell me what is going on?"

Andy sat and stared out of the window knowing this could be the end for him and Susan or emigrating. Then he thought I have nothing, no proof, nothing.

"Okay, I got offered a job as a bouncer."

"Piss off, really?" said Bobby thinking he was joking.

"Really?"

"What did you say?"

"Initially no, then I would think about it."

"Tell me you are joking?"

"No, I am not" replied Andy.

Andy then gave a full rundown on his observations on the premises and what he had learned about activities of the Smokers Club from the chargehand and the bouncer on the door. These were private monthly events. Bobby noted everything.

"Bobby, have you ever wondered why the Divisional Commander chose us for this?"

"Well, I been around for a while and you are new to all this, to give you experience?"

"Shit."

"Right smart arse gives me the reason."

"Well to give you a reason I have to ask you something" he paused

"Okay, but I need the truth" Andy continued.

"Right go for it."

"Are you a member of the lodge, a Freemason, a brother of the brotherhood?"

"No Andy, I know that Danny and Gordon are most are in the office."

"Is the Divisional Commander involved in the Lodge?"

"Well that is a strange question because I heard him say one night, he hated it as they held back good cops from gaining promotion because they were either Catholics or not part of the brotherhood"

"Okay, so I shall ask you again, why you think we were chosen for this job?"

"Aw shit Andy what is going on man" replied Bobby as the penny dropped with him.

"We are being used to destroy or bring down current and previously serving officers"

"Are you joking?"

"Nope."

"This could finish us Andy and I am over halfway through my service to a pension" Bobby said.

"Listen, Bobby if this goes tits up, I will take the wrap for everything you have too much to lose."

"Andy look DS Anderson has just come out of there, who is the other guy."

Andy just sat and stared as Anderson and Berger walked by the car on the opposite side of the road.

"Bobby don't ask please," said Andy in a fashion that sent shivers down Bobby's spine.

Observations continued until just after eleven o'clock when the premises closed. The doors were shut over after the last patron left. A male appeared at the front door and handed the bouncer what appeared to be a large wad of cash which he put in his pocket. "Bobby, sit tight," said Andy.

As the pubs and clubs surrounding Valentino's closed and previously premium parking spaces became vacant the street became quieter. Chip shops had the usual customers lapping up the last drops of the New Year, Chinese and Indian carry-out shops served the drunks Sweet and Sours, Curries, while the other dished up bags of Pakora. Taxis ferried the last of the masses out of the area by midnight.

"Andy do you fancy an early night and we can see the Divisional Commander at seven at the dump?"

"Bobby, what is missing here?"

"Dunno"

"The girls and the Jeep?"

"Christ, I forgot about them"

"Not a good idea Bobby," said Andy

At eleven-thirty that evening the first of the cars arrived. "Andy do you see what I see"

"Yep"

The cars came and went throughout the night arriving on the half-hour and leaving on forty-five minutes. About four fifteen the last of the cars departed as Jeanna and Angelina appeared on the street with a minder. The Jeep arrived and took them away. Andy watched as the bouncer closed the premises.

"Bobby, the Children's Home asap mate. Bobby sped their car down the road. Not once encountering the jeep which probably returned via the motorway. As they sat and waited, they assembled their report for the Divisional Commander. The saw the headlights from a vehicle turning into the street causing them to duck down low. The Jeep passed by, dropped off the girls, and made off out of the street just after six-thirty that morning

"Where have they been," said, Andy.

"God only knows" replied Bobby.

"Okay, the dump or we are going to be late."

"Good morning boys," said the Divisional Commander.

"Good morning sir handing him the sealed envelope."

"Andy, how is your good lady?"

"Fine sir thanks you, we need to talk."

"What about?" asked the boss.

"What is NOT in today's report" he emphasised.

"Bobby, I thought you were the senior detective in this job."

"I agree with Andy sir on this one sorry."

"Christ sake Okay."

"Sir here, six o'clock, plainclothes for you," said Andy.

"Who do you think you are Blackmore" barked the Divisional Commander.

"Andy Blackmore sir," he said with a smile.

"I should have known better than get you involved in this" he replied as if ready to burst a blood vessel.

"Sir I know what your end game is here, just trust me and Bobby please."

"Bobby, I trust you as a worthy seasoned Detective. Blackmore, I would not trust you with my wife."

"That has been said by many before sir, but you are fine there" he replied smiling with a nod.

The Divisional Commander, known for his liking of strong mints in the morning nearly choked on the one he had in his mouth. The three parted company.

Bobby and Andy headed home for a well-deserved sleep.

"Do you know something Andy you have to learn to respect rank in this job"

"Do you know something Bobby respect is earned, not a privilege"

"See you at the dump I shall walk down and get you there," said Andy

"No problem," said Bobby watching Andy leave the car

Bobby drove off and as a veteran detective thinking back on all the young bucks he had as Acting Detective Constables he had never come across anyone like this one and ringing in his ears was Andy's parting words of earning respect for rank. He was gaining a lot of respect for Andy because of his demeanour and his "who gives a shit attitude". Bobby decided to look at himself and maybe adopt a bit of Andy for himself. That was the beauty of this job he thought, take a little bit of the best of everyone.

Andy put the key into the Yale lock and went into the flat quietly. He went over to the cupboard and drew out his brandy glass. It was just after seven-thirty in the morning, corn flakes, coco pops, tea and toast were being served or made all over the country, Andy was pouring a large Brandy for himself. As he sipped the brandy he looked out on the dark sky and the stars on a winter's morning from the dark living room as he got comfortable on his large couch.

"Andy, Andy," said Susan quietly shaking him.

"Andy bedtime for you" as she took the glass from his hand.

A dazed and confused Andy staggered into the bedroom and slept until his alarm went off at five o'clock.

"Susan" he shouted but got no reply, as a matter of urgency he put the kettle on before heading into the shower.

Showered and in his towel, he called the Berger household.

"Hello."

"Brian is Susan there."

"Yes, she is."

"Great can I have a quick word please."

"She was saying you have had your shifts changed Andy why is that?"

"No big deal just an enquiry into housebreakings Brian so can you get me, Susan, please."

"Sorry, she is busy" as the phone was hung up.

Andy's head went into overdrive as he made an urgent telephone call.

"Hello."

"Alice it is Andy here."

"Oh, right, how are you?"

"Good Alice but I need mega favour."

"Okay, go for it," she said listening to Andy.

"Hello," said Brian Berger

"Hi, this is Alice a friend of Susan's is she there please."

"Certainly, hang on please."

"Susan call for you" shouted her father.

"Hello, Susan here,

"Hi Alice," she said recognising her voice immediately.

"Susan listen say nothing, Andy phoned looking for you a few minutes ago your dad refused to let him speak to you Andy called me to let you know."

"Oh, that is great honey thank you see you soon," said Susan as she hung up.

"Who was that," asked her dad

"One of the girls from work, we have a night out arranged."

"Good, get you away from him for a night."

Six o'clock Bobby and Andy met at the Dump run by the council. It was winter hours in operation, so it was closed from four o'clock. The Divisional Commanders personal car pulled up and he got out. Andy looked at him.

"Spread them, sir, please"

"You better be joking Blackmore" was the retort.

"Nope"

"Bobby?"

"Do as he says sir, please"

Their Divisional Commander stood in a rubbish dump run by the council with his legs spread and his arms outstretched being searched by his Detectives. He was searched thoroughly.

"Sir here is what you did not have in your report," Andy said out in the open air in case the car was bugged. Andy gave "the boss" the full story everything that happened the night before.

"I am so sorry sir we had to do what we did earlier, but we are shitting it to be honest," said Bobby

"You guys are brilliant, stick with it for five more days please you know it is just us in this mess?" requested the Divisional Commander.

Bobby and Andy both responded with a nod.

When Andy got home, he went into the bedroom quietly and saw that Susan had returned home and was safely tucked up in bed. After the response, he got from Brian Berger when he had tried to contact Susan, he was not sure if she would be back that evening.

Over the next five days Bobby and Andy stuck to their task North, South, East and West repeated itself, the loci were the same on each occasion.

At the end of the mission, the last sealed envelope was handed over to the Divisional Commander.

"Sir, Bobby and I were wondering, where does this go now?"

"I shall be in touch and thank you both, oh did you know I retire on Thursday," he said without answering the question asked of him.

"No Sir," said Bobby.

"Drinks my office by invite."

"Not much chance of us being there then."

"See ya guys," said the boss with a smile as he drove off for the last time.

"What is that all about Bobby?"

"Christ only knows" replied Andy.

"What shift are we meant to be."

"Same answer Andy."

Bobby and Andy melted back into the CID room and got on with their daily work, Andy once again started to look at the wilful fire-raising and the vandalisms along with the daily filing. The days passed by until it was time for the big retirement.

That Thursday the Divisional Commander walked into the CID room before his official retirement reception. He summoned everyone to be present in the room. He waited patiently as each of the detective officers DI. O'Dowd DS. Anderson Danny, Gordon, Bobby, and Andy waited on him to speak to them. Gentlemen my room please, in fact, the meeting room. You shall all want to be present at this one. He said looking at Bobby and Andy in particular.

A large gathering of uniformed and civilian staff, the controllers, the typists, even the traffic wardens were present. A large spread of food and drinks had been laid on for all and sundry.

Looking resplendent in his uniform the Divisional Commander entered the room for the last time to loud applause which visibly shook him, followed by the CID officers.

An Assistant Chief Constable had made an appearance at the office from Force Headquarters to wish the Divisional Commander a fond farewell after over thirty years of service to the community. In the end, it came down to the Deputy Divisional Commander to make the farewell speech which he did with great success praising the Divisional Commanders rise through the ranks regaling in his successes and failures along the way information that had been sent in by his colleagues and former colleagues to much hilarity.

It was now the turn of the Divisional Commander himself to make his farewell speech. He stood there surveying his audience for a moment. There was an eerie silence about the place. In a very soft and endearing voice, the Divisional Commander started his farewell speech...

"Ladies and Gentlemen. Thank you for attending. Do you know something, this is the best Division I have ever been in, there is something very special about this office and Division, it is like a family and that is something I have never experienced in thirty years of service, everyone here today has for me, been a joy to work with and I am not just saying that. Today, of all days, I am going to give my final press conference, probably one of the saddest. All shall be revealed later today."

Four unknown officers entered the room effectively barring the egress doors. Their presence did not go unnoticed by the retiring officer and he nodded to them in recognition.

"To you all, I thank you for your loyalty to me and the job. All I have to say is, goodbye from me"

There was loud applause as 'the boss' accepted handshakes all around. DS Anderson left the room quietly with two of the officers who arrived earlier

Flanked by a press officer, Chief Superintendent Burch was about to make his last press conference in front of the cameras and the nations media on something that would blow the lid off everything locally, possibly nationally, the abuse of children in care.

Susan sat on the couch at home watching the Scottish News unfold with it's usual "what happened that day". The announcer said they were going live to Z Divisional Police HQ for a live broadcast, she watched intently as the cameras focussed in on Divisional Commander Burch while waiting on Andy getting home.

The television controllers and producers were giving signals that they were ready to go live any time, producers were relaying information back to the studios. The Divisional Commander was sitting waiting looking for the live feed into the homes of millions then a female with a clipboard appeared in front of him. 3' 2' 1' GO was the signal.

"Ladies and Gentlemen, I am Chief Superintendent Burch' Divisional Commander of Z Division. Today I retire from the police after over thirty years of service. My parting gift to you all is, that, at this time, senior police officers serving and retired, councillors, local political figures and others are being detained as I speak to you concerning the alleged sexual abuse of children in care. I want to thank two of my officers, who I shall refer to as Officer A and Officer B who have sacrificed their family time, to expose all this alleged wrongdoing to children in the care system. I handpicked two officers I trusted to confirm the information I had. They came through one hundred per cent for me so to A and B thank you. You know who you are. I thank you from the bottom of my heart. When I started in this job over thirty years ago, I believed wholeheartedly in this job. I believed that we were here to guard, watch and patrol. To protect society, to watch and patrol the areas we were given to serve. Yet some have chosen to abuse their position, a select few that bring these wonderful police service into disrepute. To the parents of the children, we have failed I sincerely apologise, having said that, I only became aware of what was happening recently. I am not taking any questions from the media; this statement is my last statement as I retire in one hour. Ladies and Gentlemen of the press, I thank you and wish you all the best for the future".

At that Burch rose from his table for the last time, exiting stage right, ignoring the barrage of questions being asked by reporters. The cameras cut away back to the newsroom.

Andy and Bobby watched the live broadcast on the Tv in the staff canteen. They said nothing about the contents of the speech as the canteen was full of officers from other departments who were astounded by the revelations.

"Bobby," said an officer from the Divisional Intelligence Office "Who are the officers Burch was referring to?" he asked, "We know absolutely nothing about this enquiry in our office, what is the point of having an intelligence office and hide things?" he asked sounding a little perturbed.

Bobby shrugged his shoulders before looking back at the Tv screen.

As Andy reached his flat, he was praying Susan had missed the broadcast, if not, he was in for some tough questions from her. The very second, he stepped into the living room his worst fears were realised, Susan was waiting for him as she stood with her hands on her hips having heard the door close.

"Hiya," he said kissing her on her cheek "Are you okay?" he asked looking at her

"Well, am I okay? that depends on your answers" she replied.

"To what?"

"Officer A and Officer B, Officer A for Andy and Officer B for Bobby, I saw the live broadcast, Andy," she said.

He said nothing but nodded in the affirmative looking directly into her eyes.

"Well done you, I am so proud of you." She hugged him tightly before they both sat down.

At that moment, the telephone began to ring continuously."

"Okay, who is going to answer it," said Andy.

"I am comfortable" so not me," said Susan.

The answering machine activated. "I am sorry neither Andy nor Susan is available to take your call at this time that doesn't mean they are not at home they just don't want to speak to you please leave a message for either of us."

"When did you change that message," said Susan laughing.

"When you moved in," he replied cheekily.

"Susan, its mum call me please, now or when you get in."

"Mum," said Susan as she leapt from the couch grabbing at the phone.

"Susan can you get back here tonight please."

"What's wrong mum?" Asked Susan.

"Please get here" she replied with her voice quivering.

"Okay, calm down I shall be there soon" replied Susan trying not to get anxious.

Susan was concerned about the tone in her mother's voice she knew something was wrong at home.

"Andy, I have to go" and find out what is wrong with mum" by the sound of it something is wrong, I have never heard her speak like that before."

"Do you want me to come with you?" he asked.

"No" I shall be fine I won't be too long" she responded.

"Okay, you take care," he said.

Andy's thoughts were, was Brian, or were Brian and Sandra caught up in the scandal? He would soon find out that is for sure.

Chapter Five

A s the night wore on Andy heard nothing from Susan which worried him as he feared that her father had been caught up in the child abuse scandal that was about to erupt all around the city. As he put the lights out in the flat and ready to go to his bed alone, the door opened into the hallway and Susan appeared with her mum carrying an overnight bag.

"Andy can mum stay here tonight?"

"Yes, of course, she can."

Andy knew then that the worst-case scenario had happened, and that Brian had been scooped up in the enquiry he had been part of for the last couple of weeks. He was also sure that the Valentino Club was his downfall, then again maybe not. What of DS Anderson, he thought having seen him leave the Divisional Commanders retirement party in the company of two unknowns.

The telephone rang late into the night, it was the night shift controller from the office,

"Andy?" he asked.

"Yes."

"Andy, we have made a massive error here you and Bobby have been given tomorrow off then back in at 0800hrs the following morning."

"Hey, thanks that's the best news all day."

"What was that Andy?" said, Susan inquisitively.

"Day off tomorrow."

"Brilliant means you can look after mum."

"Yeah fine"

"Okay, what is happening Sandra and why are you here?"

"I think you know why Andy and I just can't go into it tonight please."

"No problem."

"Susan you be with your mum tonight I shall move into the small box room with the fold-down bed."

"Andy no I shall go there," said, Sandra.

"Okay, if you wish the bed is clean never been used and the linen is fresh."

"That is all I need."

Susan was in a daze at the news her father had been detained as part of the enquiry along with approximately twenty others including two females. All she could think about was the massive effect on her and her future if her father were named but she knew that under Scots law his name would not go public immediately. She sat and spoke with Andy as to the best way forward. It was decided that she should go to school and say nothing until they found out what was happening with her father.

Just after eight o'clock in the morning, Susan went into the staff room and the only topic was the news from the previous evening which was headline news on all the newspapers. The door to the staff room opened and in walked the Head of the school. "ladies and gentlemen as you are aware, we have had a few trying days in this school and to add to that we had the news last night which may or may not involve some of the pupils here. I am requesting that this is not discussed at all but if a pupil approaches you with information please refer them to me. Thank you" he said leaving the staffroom without further comment. Susan did not join in the conversation but busied herself with some paperwork she required for staff.

As Andy was making breakfast for Sandra and himself in the flat, she wandered into the living room.

"Morning Andy."

"Morning Sandra," he said without turning around. "What can I get you?"

"Tea and toast will do please, in fact, can you do me scrambled eggs?" she asked

"Yes, of course, I can" he replied reaching into the cupboard and taking a couple of eggs from the box.

Within minutes later Sandra had tea with toast and scrambled eggs to the side on a plate in front of her. Andy had decided he would have the same as that was just as easy to make. They sat opposite each other at the table just as he and Susan had done day after day.

"Andy this is a mess."

"Do you know anything at all about what is going on Sandra."

"Honestly no I just thought he was going out with his friends or seeing another woman"

"Why would you think he was seeing someone else."

"Because as I said to you before he does not come near me and hasn't for years and he was trying to set you and I up so that he could get you out of Susan's life he was desperate for you to have sex with me then there would be no way back for you."

"Why?" asked Andy softly while looking at her.

"You know too much about him now that is why."

"The final throw of the dice was getting you to the club, you were getting set up there also. He had that all planned with a young girl, she is over sixteen now. Susan would see the photos and you would be gone, maybe even lose your job. She was a former pupil of Susan's so Susan would recognise you and her and he would say you were having an affair."

"How far has this plan gone Sandra?"

"He couldn't find the girl he wanted in the last couple of weeks as she is no longer in care."

"Do you know her name by chance."

Sandra stared into space thinking, "Something like Carrie, Kelly, Corrie, something like that."

"By any chance is it, Kerry?"

"Yes, that is it, how the hell did you know that?"

"Doesn't matter"

"Right I am going for a shave and shower you make yourself at home."

"Thank you."

As Sandra heard the bathroom door close the phone rang, she let it ring for a moment then decided to answer it,

"Hello, Susan?"

"No Brian, it is Sandra."

"Sandra, why are you not here?"

"Because I am here away from you."

"Sandra you have to come home."

"Do I.?"

"Yes, and now I mean right now" he demanded.

"Brian have you been charged with anything."

"Get home now Sandra" he demanded again in a raised voice.

"Get lost Brian the days of you and I are over I am going to tell all."

"Stupid bitch I will get the jail and you know that, and possibly you as well for that matter."

"Yes, and I will be free of you starting now" as she hung up the phone.

"Yes, Yes, Yes" she shouted so loud Andy opened the bathroom door wrapped in a towel

"Sandra, what the hell? the whole street must have heard you"

"Good, this is my day of freedom Andy" as she held out her arms wide "Freedom"

"Geezuz Andy is that an offensive weapon you have under that towel," she said laughing

"Sandra get a grip you are the mother of my fiancée."

"Sorry, Andy it is just, oh forget it."

"Andy tell me something I have been told that every young guy's dream is an older woman."

"Not their future mother in law, well not for me."

"Shame, because I am going to have that one way or another."

"Don't think so" as he went back into the bathroom which was filled with steam from the running shower slamming the door behind him and locking it.

Sandra was looming around the living room in her dressing gown, she turned on the radio. The music filled the room for a few moments until the announcer said that they were breaking away for the news at ten o'clock.

"This is the news at ten," said the announcer. "Following several arrests concerning an ongoing abuse enquiry several people have been charged and shall appear in court on Monday. Our information is that several others have been released without charge pending further enquiries. More arrests are expected over the weekend".

"Sandra's immediate thought was that Brian was either cleared or pending further enquiry"

She picked up the phone and called home.

"Brian, cleared or pending further enquiry?"

"None of your business" was his reply.

"Thank you, get a lawyer, I am gone."

"You can't" he demanded.

"Oh yes I can," said she. then paused for a moment.

"Tell you what, I shall make it easy for you divorce me for adultery, you were witness to a load of that over the times we went to your club, I am going to destroy you, this is "kiss and tell time" to a national newspaper on the back of the police enquiry or a cash settlement" as she slammed down the phone.

Andy's phone rang continuously and went to the answering machine. As Andy was in the shower, he only heard the phone ringing as Sandra was cancelling out the calls. She knew they were from Brian.

Sandra headed back to the bedroom to lay out her clothes she would wear that day passing the bathroom. She heard the shower running and temptation got the better of her despite everything that told her it was wrong, she tried to open the door which she found to be locked much to her disappointment.

"Sandra the shower is free now" shouted Andy a few minutes later.

"Okay, thank you, have you left the shower on" she replied from the bedroom.

"Yes."

"Great thanks" she replied.

Sandra slipped into the shower wishing Andy was in there with her, but she knew that he would not succumb to her charms unlike nearly all of Susan's previous boyfriends. Sandra had a secret love for younger guys with their stamina and virility and Andy was a target for her.

When Andy was getting dressed and with Sandra in the shower Andy heard the main door being opened.

"Andy" shouted Susan "I have got the rest of the day off" as she came through the door.

"Brilliant news we can go out for something to eat then and take your mum with us."

"Where is she?"

"In the shower" he replied.

Susan heard the shower being turned off and her mum going to her room to get dressed. She waited until she got into the living room.

"Oh," said Sandra on seeing Susan in the living room, "When did you get home?" she asked

"Just a few minutes ago when you were in the shower" Susan replied.

"Mum have you heard from Dad?" she asked.

"Yes, he called me this morning he is at home."

"So, are you going home today then?"

"Not yet I can't" she answered in a quiet voice and shaking her head.

"Okay, I understand."

"How long do you think you will be here for?"

"I am going to make arrangements to get rented accommodation for the moment."

"This is terrible mum," said Susan

"Do you know I might even just go away for a few weeks of sunshine."

"Well if you can afford it why not."

Sandra pondered the idea of a holiday without her husband and decided that it would be good for her and let her plan for a future without him one way or another. She also gave thought to what had gone on in her past life with him and the way that he had used and abused her using her as nothing more than a sex toy for his gratification while all the time hiding behind his uniform to make himself a respected member of the community. She thought about bringing it all crashing down and finishing him off once and for all. She also knew it could be the beginning of the end for her also.

"How was school Susan?" asked Sandra

"It was okay everyone was talking about the arrests and that maybe some from the school would be involved because we have quite a lot of kids there that are in care, but nobody came forward thankfully. What worries me is that dads name is linked to all this as it would finish off my career as a teacher."

"Why," said Sandra.

"Are you kidding mum think about it, me working with kids and, and, I can't even say it."

"Oh, dear Susan honestly I never thought about it."

"Right guys what are we doing pub dinner or getting a carry-out," said Andy.

"Oh, bugger it lets go for the pub I need out and a drink," said Susan.

In the pub and seated Andy looked up at the staff standing chatting and immediately saw Kerry with the others. He went to the bar and ordered a round of drinks for Sandra, Susan, and himself. He sensed Kerry watching him and looked in her direction and nodded with a smile. The other waitresses were looking over at him and giggling as Kerry whispered something to them.

Kerry walked over and stopped next to Andy placing her tray on the bar. Susan was watching the move closely and Andy's response to Kerry.

"Mum see the waitress standing next to Andy she was a former pupil of mine."

"That is nice that you managed to educate her to waitress level."

"She is going to university soon."

"Oh really" replied Sandra.

"Yes really."

"Well done her."

"Yes, she spent most of her life in care homes and foster homes."

"Well, that is fantastic for her to get a university place."

Andy came back to the table with the drinks and sat down as Susan and Sandra chatted girl talk.

"So, Andy what was your new admirer chatting to you about?"

"Eh?" was his reply.

"Kerry, what was she talking to you about?"

Andy flashed a look at Sandra knowing what hearing that name would mean to her or possibly mean to her.

"Susan what is the name of that girl."

"What girl?"

"The waitress that was in care and foster homes."

"Kerry, Kerry Ferguson, why do you ask?"

"No reason darling" as she looked at Andy.

Each of the waitresses had their tables to serve and Kerry noticed that Andy and Susan had sat in her area. She had no idea who the other person was with them. All Kerry knew was that she was seriously attracted to Andy and glad that they had sat at her table. She was also watching Susan and her interaction with Andy.

"Hi guys two days in a row I must be doing something right to get you back so soon," said Kerry.

"Well, it was Andy's idea to come here as he said the waitresses were cute" laughed Susan.

"Oh Miss, oh I mean Susan, not Miss, You know what I mean anyway orders please."

"Kerry this is my mum, Sandra."

"Pleased to meet you Susan's mum."

"I have heard a lot about you Kerry" as she stared at her.

"You are a star in Susan's eyes."

"Well you daughter was, or should I say is my inspiration."

"Really?" Said, Sandra looking at Kerry.

"Can I take your order?" she asked.

"Yes sure," said Andy who was observing the exchanges between Sandra and Kerry.

Kerry took their order and returned to the kitchen oblivious to the fact that she was speaking to Sandra Berger, wife of Brian Berger, at that time she gave it no thought at all.

She went back into the bar area and stood with her tray at the ready for the next orders. Suddenly, a sense of dread came over Kerry, Susan Berger, Sandra Berger, names she had heard before from someone while in care. She looked over at the table and saw Andy watching her. Kerry knew that he knew the connection. Kerry looked at Sandra who was talking to Susan, but flashing looks at her. Kerry felt very uncomfortable.

Andy went to the bar as Kerry took an order from a table. Andy had intentionally placed himself next to the "staff only" area.

"Andy."

"Yes, Kerry.?"

"Nothing."

"No Kerry, that is not the answer I am looking for."

"Andy what do you work as. "

"Kerry, I am a police officer. I thought you knew that?" he said surprised.

"Oh, Christ no" she replied.

"Kerry I am on your side I have to ask you to stay on my side Kerry please," he said as if pleading with her.

"Now when you get back to the table, we have been speaking about the bands coming in here."

"Okay," she replied.

Andy returned to the table carrying their drinks. Kerry arrived with their starters on a tray.

Susan noticed a change in Kerrys' demeanour as she watched the interaction between Andy and Kerry, Sandra was watching Kerry like a hawk for different reasons and wondered if this was the Kerry her husband had been looking for, she was ninety-nine per cent positive.

"Andy, can I ask you something?" Said Susan

"Sure."

"Do you fancy Kerry?"

A question that surprised her mother who said nothing

"No, by asking that you are out of order" he replied.

"Sorry, Andy I am."

Andy whispered into her ear "let this go until we get to the flat please."

Susan looked at Andy curiously.

"Please trust me he whispered."

"Okay," she replied "Your eyes are all over the place" she continued.

"Yep," said Andy.

Later, another waitress cleared away the plates from the starters, Sandra saw Kerry go into the toilet and excused herself from the table heading right into the toilet behind her. There were four cubicles in the toilets only one was closed over with the red locked sign initiated.

Sandra waited outside the cubicle leaning against the sinks. She heard the toilet being flushed and prepared herself as the door was unlocked. Kerry and Sandra stood face to face.

"Kerry, do you know who I am?"

"Yes, I do Susan's mum." She replied turning on the tap at the sink to wash her hands

"Do you know my husband Brian Berger?"

"No way the cop guy?" said, Kerry.

"Yes, the cop guy as you say."

"Mrs. Berger, I had no idea he was Susan's dad honest."

"But you knew he was married?"

"Yes."

"And that meant nothing to you did it?"

"No, he paid well, and I was young and just wanted the money."

"What do you mean young.?"

"I was young, that is what I mean."

"What age bitch?" asked Sandra becoming angrier and raising her voice.

"Fourteen."

"How much were you getting."

"Two hundred and fifty pounds a time, he loved it."

"Oh, dear God, you poor girl as she wrapped her arms around Kerry, I am so sorry."

"This is not your fault Kerry now listen to me please I need you to talk to Andy."

"No way he is a cop."

"Kerry tell him everything please save others from going through what you have."

"Don't know?" said Kerry.

"You are going to talk to Andy whether you like it or not, do you know why?"

"No."

"Because I want to see Brian Berger and all the others involved jailed for a long time, Kerry, they were wrong in what they did."

"Now go out and do your job, Kerry."

Sandra returned to the table and made her excuses for taking her time in the toilets, She stared at Andy who had seen her and Kerry leaving the toilet together. Susan went to the bar and ordered drinks, then she became engaged in some chat with people she knew.

"Kerry is going to talk to you, Andy."

"What about?"

"Everything and everyone."

"You have lost me, Sandra."

"Brian has been having sex with her since she was fourteen."

Andy sat and stared at Sandra before asking if she knew what she was getting herself into and possibly Susan. Sandra said that she did, and they would have to speak to Susan and get her feelings on the matter. Sandra looked up and saw her daughter happily chatting to friends at the bar, she wondered if they would still be friends when this was all over.

"When are you back at work?"

"Tomorrow and Sunday morning why?"

"Just asking" replied Sandra thinking about her next move

"See while Susan is at the bar can I ask something Sandra you don't have to answer."

"Okay," was her reply as she looked at him.

"How the hell did you two get into this god-awful mess."

Sandra sat silently for a few moments then began., speaking a low voice so that others in the vicinity would not eavesdrop.

"Years ago, after Susan was born, Brian started to associate with several people who moved in different circles away from the lodge where he had been a member since he was eighteen as his father was a former Master of the Lodge. For years he went out with his friends on a Friday on his own and I wasn't bothered. We went out one night and Brian suggested we meet up with a few special friends of his. We went to this club in the suburbs of the west end, People were having sex all over the place and Brian suggested I took one of the young guys. I didn't want to but then everything just took over the drink, the sex, everything we were a bit younger then but not a lot as Susan was in her late teens then and heading for university. I was already there, then I got involved sexually with "Goughie," Sheena Gough I mean it was my first lesbian affair and it was amazing as Brian had lost interest in me. Now I know he preferred younger ones a lot younger, we continued to go to the club, he would choose the younger members as they were known and I would go for the boys who were sixteen plus and came from care homes or had been in the homes. They loved the mature women like me and see sitting here telling you this I am so ashamed of everything"

"So, Sandra is that why you used to have Susan's boyfriends when she was younger?"

"Yes, I loved it."

"Is that how Brian got rid of them?"

"Yes."

"Does she know?"

"No."

"Okay,"

"And where do I fit into all this with you Sandra?"

"We have to break this cycle, Andy, I have to get away."

"Susan is coming back over Sandra," said Andy looking over her shoulder.

When Susan returned to the table and asked what they had been talking about. Andy said they had been talking about when she was young, and her mum had been filling him in about her life as a child. As they finished their meal they stayed on for a few drinks before heading back to the flat. Sandra bought two bottles of wine from the local licensed premises en route.

Back at the flat Sandra opened a bottle of wine and set out three glasses.

"None for me Sandra thank you," said Andy "I am working at eight tomorrow morning."

"Oh, Andy just a little one for a toast to us."

"Alright but not a lot."

Sandra handed out the glasses of wine and proposed a toast to a new future for them all. She then announced that she was going to see Brian and reach an agreement with him for their separation. Susan admitted that she was heartbroken about the mess her mum and dad were in, but she understood why she was leaving. They agreed that Susan would go with her mother in the morning while Andy was at work.

Andy's thoughts returned to police mode as he recalled the discussion he had about the fires and the vandalisms. What Andy was unsure about was the reception that he and Bobby would get from his fellow officers who were connected and friends of some of those arrested.

On Saturday morning Andy reported for duty. DS Anderson led the briefing, Andy was surprised to see him there, maybe more confused than surprised considering he had witnessed Anderson with Berger going into Valentinos together. Where does he fit into all this? thought Andy. At the end of the briefing, DS Anderson asked to see Andy and Bobby privately in his office.

"Come in gentlemen"

"Thanks, boss," said Bobby as they stood looking at each other.

"Close the door at your back."

DS Anderson held out his hand to shake the hands of Andy and Bobby which confused both. He congratulated them on their successful venture and helping to secure the arrests and detentions of a vast number of people involved in the scandal that was all over the newspapers. He also added that he was aware that the Divisional Commander was delighted with everything that had been done and it had been noted in their records.

"Now lads you both saw me leave with two men from the retiral the other day I cannot go into detail why I was with them, but I can assure you it was strictly police business about the enquiry. What I can say is that because of your links to Brian Berger Andy we had to be sure everything went smoothly I hope that you understand."

"Yes Sergeant."

"Normal service resumed then and enquiries to get on with," said Anderson.

"Yes, oh good luck with the fire enquiry Andy."

"Thanks, Sergeant." He replied with a smile and a nod of his head.

When they returned into the Detective Constables office they immediately sensed the atmosphere was very subdued.

"Andy, Bobby," said Danny as Gordon looked up and just nodded at them.

Andy went over and put the kettle on and offered to make everyone tea or coffee as he did at the start of every shift since starting.

"Tea all around as usual or does anyone want coffee."

"No thanks not for us," said Gordon briefly glancing up then back onto his paperwork.

Bobby looked at Andy in that "say nothing" look he could give. Each of the officers sat going through the crime reports they had been allocated to investigate with only a grunt or a groan thrown in for good measure.

"Danny and I are going out Bobby, we have a few houses to visit," said Gordon only speaking to Bobby as if he had to.

"No problem," said Bobby staring at Andy across the desk.

"Looks and feels like we have upset the apple cart, Bobby," said Andy.

"This could just be the start" was his reply.

"Andy what are you doing with those crime reports spread out on the floor."

"Looking for more clues Bobby but I know where I am going with them."

"Really?"

"Yes really, sometimes the obvious gets completely missed and it has."

Andy sat down at his desk and started phoning around the sub-divisional offices and speaking to the officers who had attended the fires and raised the crime reports. The ones he could not get he would wait until they started late shift. Andy sat and scribbled down the dates of the fires then checked back on the calendar from the previous year.

"Bobby, did you know all those fires occurred on a Wednesday?"

"No."

"Do you know that they all occurred between ten and Midnight?"

"Yes."

"I have to go back to the complainers' Bobby."

"Do you want me to come with you.?"

"No, I shall be fine I just want to go over old ground that is all."

Andy grabbed a set of car keys and set off on his own. DS Anderson entered the office.

"Bobby, have you let him loose on his own?"

"Yes Sergeant."

"Fine" he replied as he walked away.

Andy returned a few hours later with his crime reports.

"How did you get on?" asked Bobby.

"Great thanks just a couple of more things to check out then see what happens."

"Good lad," Bobby said with a smile on his face.

Andy was giving nothing away this time to anyone, but he knew he was one short step away from getting his suspect in for questioning. Andy did not have a clue his suspect had strong links to the police and for his charity work in the community.

Chapter Six

Saturday passed by with Andy updating his crime reports with little left to do other than speak to the remaining reporting officers which he did during the afternoon. A common thread appeared when he asked one of the officers who had attended two of the fires if she had seen anyone she knew at both fires.

The information he received from the officer was startling that the same person had reported both fires to the Fire Service. He gave statements to the police that he was passing the premises on fire at the time. Andy wondered why this had not been picked up along the way or was it just he had all the reports in the one place at the one time and could make the links.

"Bobby is the whisky bond open today or tomorrow?" asked Andy.

"Security is on at the weekends that is all."

"I have to find out who is in charge there."

"That is easy it is Raymond Skinner, ex-cop, good guy, did over thirty years in the job I will take you over and introduce you to him."

"Bobby who is James McCartney the local businessman."

"Geez he is big around here does a lot for charity and always on hand to help out the police with donations for the fundraising nights we have."

"Interesting."

"Why are you......." Bobby's voice trailed off as he looked at Andy

"Oh no tell me he is not your suspect; he was looked at way back when this all kicked off"

"We have to go to the bond there is one last thing I need to check out."

Andy explained that he had spoken in general to someone with a great knowledge of fire-raising and had sought advice from him and McCartney fits the profile.

"Andy you are wrong this time as his wife gave him alibis that he was at home at the time of the fires."

"He reported two of them, Bobby."

"Oh Okay."

"That is why we have to go to the bond if I am wrong, I shall admit defeat."

"Admit defeat about what asked DS Anderson."

"The fires."

"Good then file them," anybody seen Danny and Gordon?"

"They went out on enquiries hours ago" replied Bobby.

"Okay, no problem" "You two just about to finish up?"

"Yes Sergeant" replied Bobby

"I am not paying you overtime so head out."

"Where have you two been all day?"

"Enquiries Sergeant," said Danny.

"Hope you got a result then, for the time you have been out."

"Close" replied Danny.

"See you all tomorrow," said Andy.

"Yeah sure," said Bobby the other two did not reply.

Andy had been so busy doing his enquiry that he forgot about Sandra going home with Susan to confront Brian. He knew he would have to face all that when he got in. He was concerned what effect the breakup would have on Susan. Another concern was Sandra and all the information she had given him and the fact that she was making him a target for sex. Susan would go berserk if she knew what her mother was up to while she was staying with them. Susan had enough to contend with just now without that also. Then there was Kerry to add to the equation. The waters were getting murkier.

Just as Andy was about to reach his flat, he saw Kerry leaving the pub. He pulled over at the kerbside and got out of the car.

"Kerry."

"Hi, Andy."

"Kerry if you ever want to talk, I am free when you are ready."

"Thank you but how can I trust you after everything that has happened to us."

"Us?"

"Yes, us, the ones that took part in their sordid games."

"You shall be safe" he replied trying to reassure her.

"Let me think about its Andy, I am going to university to get away from all this."

Andy got back into his car and finished his journey to the flat. There was no sign of Susan's car in the street. He unlocked the door to the flat, took off his jacket and threw it onto the couch. He picked up the phone to call Susan then had second thoughts on the matter replacing it onto the cradle.

Taking the mince from the fridge he made a pot of spaghetti Bolognese, which was one of his specialities. He let it simmer with the lid on the pot ensuring that the condensation dripped back into the contents adding to the flavour. Testing the taste, he added a minute pinch of salt and then sugar to take out the sharpness of the tomatoes something not a lot of people did. Switching on the back-gas ring Andy placed a pot of water on it to bring to the boil for the spaghetti. Garlic bread went into the oven just as the door opened and in walked Susan with her mum carrying two suitcases.

"Don't worry I am not moving in" said Sandra.

"Listen stay as long as you need to" replied Andy.

"What is that? smells amazing," asked Susan.

"Spag Bog have you guys not had anything to eat?"

"No."

"I shall put more pasta on then, enough for everyone."

"Great thank you" replied Sandra who looked stressed out.

As the fresh pasta was simple and fast to cook dinner was ready to be served almost immediately. Sandra opened the remaining bottle of wine she had purchased the evening before and poured each a glass to have with their dinner. Susan returned to the living room wearing casual clothing, baggy top, and jogging pants. As they sat together Andy intentionally did not ask about the meeting but chose to say he had a good day at work in response to a question from Susan. The silent moments seemed awkward for a while but slowly and surely Sandra began to brighten up. Susan did likewise as Andy watched her knowing everything she had been through recently.

As Sandra put down her knife Andy noticed that she was not wearing her engagement, wedding, or eternity rings on her left hand. Andy lifted her left hand with his right hand and gently rubbed the third finger where her rings had been with his thumb.

"Sandra I am so sorry it has come to this."

"It is fine Andy, in effect, it is a new start for me."

"How is your mum Andy," said Susan.

"I have to call Ricky and find out the last few days have been a whirlwind with everything."

"Yes, a good idea will you be you going to see her on your days off?"

"Yes, either Monday or Tuesday when you are at school"

"Good can you take mum back home she is going to the bank with dad to get financial stuff sorted out so she can become self-sufficient?"

"Yes, certainly when have you arranged that for Sandra."

"Whenever you are available, or I can just get the bus or train," said Sandra.

"Let me call Ricky and see when they are free."

With the dinner and wine finished Susan and Sandra cleaned the plates and pots. Andy telephoned Ricky and arrangements were made for him to go see his mum on Monday morning.

"How are things between you and Alice Ricky?"

"Not great but, not bad either."

"How are the kids?"

"They get on my nerves sometimes and I come into the study out of the way."

"It is all going to take time Ricky you do know that."

"I need to get a job; we can't keep this place if I don't get a job soon."

"Can you not get a job as a chemist somewhere."

"I don't know I shall speak to some people I know who might be able to help."

"What about your other problem?"

"I am attending Gamblers Anonymous now and I have a mentor I can call."

"That is great I am pleased for you I shall see you and Alice on Monday."

"Yeah Okay she will be happy to see you."

Andy said to Sandra that everything was arranged for Monday morning and if she wanted to call Brian to confirm arrangements that would be fine. Susan said she would do it on behalf of her mother.

"Do you two mind if I go to the off licence, I think we need a little drink, Susan, after today"

"Sure, mum do you want me to go with you?" asked Susan.

"It is only along the road I need a walk to clear my head" her mother replied.

"Shall I get wine or vodka or what?"

"White or red wine shall be fine we have brandy in here anyway" replied Susan.

As the door closed Susan curled up next to Andy on the couch their special place where they shared everything. Susan gave a long sigh as she put her head on Andy's shoulder and wrapped her arm around his.

"Andy I am so sorry about all this."

"What do you mean?" he asked.

"Having all this dumped on to you on top of everything that is going on with Ricky."

"I think he is getting his act together from what he says I shall see Monday."

"Listen it is nothing to do with me, but did everything go as well as possible today."

"Yes, they are going to sort out their finances on Monday. He gave her cash today as all the bank accounts are in his name which is strange nowadays, then there is the house to sort out this shall take a while."

"Is your mum going to see about accommodation? not that there is a rush."

"Yes, that is her plan, I think she is your newest fan, to be honest."

"What makes you think that?"

"Going up in the car she was her usual jokey self-saying you came out the shower the other day wearing just a towel and she thought you were concealing an offensive weapon."

"What did you say?"

"I told her in no uncertain terms to keep her hands off it," she said laughing.

"Well, Susan I don't think that is something mum and daughter should be discussing, do you?"

"Oh, she meant no harm by it it's just her quirky style" replied Susan snuggling into Andy.

Andy was concerned about her staying over when Susan was at work and her behaviour sexually towards guys in general, particularly him.

Shortly thereafter Sandra returned to the flat carrying two bottles of wine. Andy rose from the couch and opened a bottle pouring a glass for Sandra while he and Susan each had a small brandy.

"Would either of you like to watch a romantic video?"

"Which one?"

"French Lieutenant's Woman."

"Sure, that is supposed to be a brilliant film," said Susan as Andy put the video into the machine.

"Andy pause that until I get a refill please," said Sandra pointing at the video player.

"Okay,"

Andy watched as she took the bottle of wine over beside her placing it on the coffee table.

Andy sat reading as Sandra and Susan watched the film. At eleven o'clock Andy decided he would go to bed as he was starting at eight o'clock in the morning. "Goodnight ladies he said as he left the room."

"Goodnight," said both not taking their eyes off the screen.

The following morning Andy walked into the office Danny and Gordon were sitting at their desks, Bobby followed Andy in within minutes. Briefing finished they returned to the Detective Constables room.

"See before I put the kettle on is there a problem in here," said Andy looking around the office at Danny and Gordon.

"No way," said Danny.

"Just that yesterday there seemed to be an atmosphere."

"Well," said Gordon "the problem is that a lot of people we know were caught up in the net the other day, a lot of good guys whose lives are in bits and could be going to jail when they appear in court tomorrow."

"So, are you blaming me and Bobby for this?"

"In a way, you were both part of that enquiry," said Gordon looking up at Andy.

"Yes, we were, and my stance is they were in the wrong, not us."

Danny and Gordon looked at each other.

"Now do you want tea or not?" asked Andy

"Yeah sure stick the kettle on," said Danny.

Andy felt the atmosphere starting to relax a little. What they did not know was, that it might not be over by a long shot if Kerry Ferguson stepped forward with her story.

"Bobby are we going out this morning?"

"Where are you off to Andy?" asked Danny.

"Trying to get this fire thing sorted out."

"Okay," he said with a smile as that was an old enquiry of his that he had filed.

Bobby and Andy made their way to the bonded warehouse. Bobby got out of the car to be embraced by Raymond Skinner who was always pleased to see old colleagues. Bobby introduced Andy to Raymond.

"So, Bobby what can I do for you?"

"It's Andy that needs a little information, Raymond."

"Okay, how can I help you, Andy?"

"I believe the wife of James McCartney works here," said Andy.

"Aye Rosie, cracking girl."

"See if I give you dates, and times can it be checked if she was off or here?"

"Sure, but we have to be careful."

"Andy handed Raymond the list."

"Oh, that's easy she would be here," said Raymond without referring to any other paperwork.

"How would you know that?"

"Because she always works nights during the week from nine to seven in the morning, Monday to Friday done it for years."

"Thank you, that is a great help believe me" replied Andy with a broad smile.

"Well Andy good luck with your enquiry," said Raymond as Andy and Bobby left.

In the car on the way back to the office, Andy discussed what he had in full with Bobby, and it was decided to take it back to DS Anderson to get his opinion on the enquiry although both thought there was enough to bring McCartney in for questioning.

"DS Anderson we need to speak to you," said Andy.

"Okay, hit me with it." He sat back and listened.

Andy went through everything that he had concerning the fires enquiry as DS Anderson carefully weighing up the evidence.

"Well, what are you waiting for Andy, go get him and try to encourage him to come to the office voluntarily if not section him."

As Bobby and Andy arrived at the house Bobby asked Andy to do this one as he deserved it after all the work, he had put into it.

"Mr James McCartney?" asked Andy to the man who had opened the door. He was not what Andy expected at all, a large, balding, rotund chap in his late forties unshaven and with deep-set dark eyes.

"Yes." Replied McCartney

"May we come in sir?" asked Andy producing his warrant card.

"How can I help you," McCartney asked.

"Well sir I am Acting Detective Constable Andy Blackmore and I have been investigating several fires in this area" stopping as he was interrupted by McCartney.

"Okay, how does this lead you here? other than I discovered two of them and called the emergency services to the scene."

"I would like you to come to the office for an interview about those fires."

"Jim where are you going," said Rosemary McCartney who had been at the door listening to every word.

"Looks like I am a suspect for the fires in the area."

"Officers this has been investigated and except for the two he reported he was with me," she said

"Mrs. McCartney be very very careful, or you could be coming with us also," said Andy

"Are you threatening to take my wife to the office also?" asked McCartney.

"What I am saying is she should think carefully before giving you an alibi again as that is tantamount to Attempting to Pervert the Course of Justice."

"Leave her out of this please gentlemen, I shall go with you."

"Shall we go then?" said Andy.

"Yes" replied McCartney.

On his arrival at the office, James McCartney signed the voluntary attendance book before being taken to an interview room on the ground floor. He was advised that the interview would be recorded in writing question and answer or if he wished to save time, he could make a voluntary statement under common law caution. He agreed to make a voluntary statement outwith the presence of a lawyer, and he admitted wilfully setting fire to premises in the area. He stated that he was under great strain at the time as his business was failing and he was jealous of others who were being successful. He signed each page of the statement as did Andy and Bobby.

McCartney was taken to the charge bar where he was formally cautioned and charged with all the fires. He made no reply after each charge. The duty officer who knew McCartney well said that given the circumstances and the value of the property involved he was of a mind to keep him in custody for court the following day. He also took into consideration the passage of time since the fires so he would consult the duty Procurators Fiscal. Meanwhile, Andy and Bobby took McCartney to be photographed and fingerprinted, while the duty officer made his phone call to the PF.

On his return to the charge bar, the duty officer had a decision from the PF. "Mr Boyle, the duty PF has decided that you should be released under the Bail(Scotland)Act 1980 and to report to the Sheriff Court on Friday morning at nine-thirty is that understood Mr McCartney?"

"Yes, Inspector."

"Jim I never thought I would see the day that you would be standing there."

"True neither did I Inspector and I can say I have been treated with respect by both officers today."

"That is good."

"Mr Blackmore, what is going to happen to my wife?"

"When we go up the road, I shall get her details then report her to the Procurators Fiscal let him decide as to whether he wants to charge her or not."

"Thank you."

"Right c'mon let's get you home to your wife and kids and don't forget your form."

Andy and Bobby took McCartney home. Andy explained to Rosemary McCartney the situation and what was going to be done about reporting her. She was charged with Attempting to Pervert the Course of Justice. She made no reply.

"Listen, see doing it this way keeps you with your kids" Andy paused "Thank you for your cooperation, both of you."

Andy and Bobby left the house and returned to the office where DS Anderson was waiting with Danny and Gordon.

"Well done kid that is a great result," said DS Anderson.

"Well done Andy," said, Danny.

"That goes for me also," said Gordon, patting him on his shoulder.

"Suppose I have to make the tea while you do the paperwork for this one?"

"That would be good Bobby and thanks for everything today."

"You are welcome."

A man in plainclothes entered the room, who was unknown to all in there.

"May I help you, sir?" asked Detective Sergeant Anderson.

"Sorry, let me introduce myself Chief Superintendent Ralph McGrory" he paused "Your new Divisional Commander I start here tomorrow, and I am having a look around the place."

DS Anderson introduced his team to McGrory who looked like he was early forties and he shook hands with each in turn. "So, what has been happening today then" he enquired looking at DS Anderson to which he informed the new Chief Superintendent of their success in resolving the wilful fire-raisings.

"Whose enquiry was it?"

"It was Andy Blackmore's enquiry sir," said DS Anderson.

"Actually, I had the enquiry sir, but we all chipped in," said Andy.

"Good I like teamwork."

"Oh, by the way, Mr Burch has told me about you and Bobby, and the work you have both been involved in should be interesting to see how far that gets, kids against cops and businessmen, interesting."

"Goodbye gentlemen," he said leaving the room.

"Nice to meet you, sir," said DS Anderson.

Andy looked at Bobby and Bobby knew it was because of the comment that was made as DS Anderson left the room returning about ten minutes later.

"Listen up you lot I just made a phone call our new Divisional Commander is forty-three years of age, fifteen years police service and was brought up through the office system at Force Headquarters. two years' probation then identified as a highflyer after his promotion exams, not been on the street for the past eleven years. A stickler for the rules and said to be heading for the top of the tree in the next few years" said DS Anderson "Oh and well connected so be careful."

"Andy is all your paperwork done for the fires."

"Yes, Sergeant everything has been updated."

"Right, there is just fifteen minutes to go so you are as well going up the road. On Wednesday you will be on your own as its Bobby's day off then back together on Thursday will you be Okay?"

"Well, soon find out Sergeant."

"Yes, we will, and make sure you get the reports for the fires and the Attempt to Pervert to the Fiscals office on time."

The phone rang on Danny's desk, "Danny here, Aye he is here" he was heard to say.

"Andy, it is an external call for you," he said handing the receiver to Andy.

"Andy?" Said a female voice.

"Yes."

"Andy it is Kerry Ferguson."

"Hi, Kerry."

"Hi Andy, Andy I am going to St Andrew's University and I want to leave all this in the past who is going to believe us anyway, but what I will do for you is tell you everything I know and who was involved that I know of, it is all I want to do," she said in a gentle tone.

"Okay, Kerry I respect your decision we can arrange a meeting here on Wednesday night I start at six o'clock."

"No Andy, away from the office please."

"Okay, I shall be in touch in the next few days."

"Everything okay Andy?" asked Bobby looking at the disappointment on Andy's face.

"On the one hand no on the other hand yes."

"What does that mean" asked DS Anderson.

"It means I have a decision to make on someone's future happiness that lies elsewhere."

"Geez, you speak in riddles when you are hiding something."

"See you Wednesday," he said leaving the room.

Andy sat in his car pondering the phone call from Kerry then went back into the office.

"Sergeant can I have a word please"

"My shift is a late shift on Wednesday, can you arrange for June to be in plain clothes to come with me to meet someone."

"About what?"

"The enquiry Bobby and I were involved in and for that matter you also."

"I was not involved in that enquiry."

"Okay if you say so."

"What time do you need her here?"

"Six o'clock please."

"Okay, I shall arrange it, this better be good Blackmore."

"Could be Sergeant, have to wait and see."

"Andy drove to the flat, opened the door and could smell home cooking coming from the kitchen."

"Hey, girls, I am home."

"Hi, Andy" shouted Sandra.

"Susan" he called out but got no reply.

"Susan will be back shortly Andy, so I have made dinner just waiting on her returning"

"No problem," he said.

"Where has she gone?"

"Oh, her friend at the pub wanted some advice so she is away down there at the moment."

"Oh right."

"I will put the steaks on when she gets in hopefully soon everything else is almost ready."

Just at that Susan came into the flat.

"Hello Andy," she said kissing him on the cheek.

"How was your day?"

"Good" he replied, "Were you at the pub?"

"Yes, Kerry wanted to speak to me she wanted advice about University and a few other things."

"Well, she could not ask anyone better."

"Steaks are on Susan keep an eye on them while I go to the bathroom," said Sandra.

"Andy come here what is going on with you and Kerry? she asked me to give you this" handing him a note.

"I shall explain later I need to speak to you alone."

"Okay, this better be plausible."

"Wow, that was great Sandra I was starving" as he finished dinner.

"You are welcome, Andy."

"Susan, I know that it is Sunday, but do you fancy the gym for an hour"

"Yes, that would be great" she replied.

"Or even a brisk walk."

"Even better, Mum what about you?"

"No chance I shall be here when you get back off you two go."

Once out of the flat Susan asked Andy again what was going on between him and Kerry and he explained to her that he had got a phone call at the office from her and she wanted to speak to him privately about certain things before she left for university. He said that he had asked for June to be there with him as he always wanted a female officer with him.

Susan told Andy that when she was with Kerry she seemed uneasy and not her usual self as if she was hiding something, that is when she handed me the note to her for you to meet her at the end of her shift at 7 pm on Wednesday along at the bus stop. Andy said to Susan as this was a police issue, she could not mention the meeting to anyone including her mother. She agreed.

On the short walk back to the flat Andy wondered what information Kerry held and was he able to keep it to himself. If nothing else it would be a goldmine of intelligence, as she appeared to have been involved in everything for a few years at least. He knew that he would have to be careful especially after the comment made by the new Divisional Commander.

Chapter Seven

Andy awoke to a space in the bed beside him. Eight Forty-Five said the clock on the bedside table. Susan had slipped out of bed leaving him alone and had already left for school. He rolled onto his back staring at the ceiling wondering what Kerry may tell of her life in the children's home. His mind rolled over the questions that he wanted to ask but decided while lying there to let her just tell her story without interrupting. He also knew that he would have June by his side or at least he hoped his DS Anderson had got it arranged. He rubbed his bleary eyes and sat up in bed looking around himself. He began to gather his thoughts slowly and trying to get away from the enquiry.

Andy knew that he had to take Sandra back to her matrimonial home to see Brian and all that was going to unfold there. He also knew that he had to go see Ricky and Alice and was hoping that their life was getting back on track. Andy heard the door to the shower cabinet closing in the bathroom and the water running. He got up and pulled on his dressing gown and began to make his way into the living room. Passing the bathroom, the door was open Sandra was in the shower, the steam was clinging to the glass and the condensation was running down into the shower tray. The outline of her naked body was visible.

Andy was sitting at the table sipping his morning coffee, his toast with strawberry jam lying beside it. He looked out of the window, the morning was typically wintery and dank. Streetlights were still on, cars were nose to tail, workers heading out to start their day and parents taking children to the local school all adding to the chaos on the road, headlights going one way, taillights going the other. What Andy did know was that he was not heading for the building site as nothing would be getting done and no money earned.

"Andy" "Andy," said Sandra wakening him out of his trance-like state. Andy looked over at Sandra.

"Good morning, the kettle is boiled," he said beckoning over to the kettle with a raise of his eyebrow and a shake of his head before returning his gaze out of the window. Sandra poured a coffee and returned to the table.

Andy looked at Sandra, her dressing gown was, as usual, loosely tied at the waist. Her cleavage was exposed and evocative almost seductive, her hair dishevelled from a quick towel dry but, today there was something different about her whole demeanour. She was quiet, she was withdrawn, she looked like someone who was facing a death sentence and heading for the gallows. The bold, brassy Sandra was gone, for today at least.

"What's up?" said Andy.

"Nothing" she replied looking down into her cup.

"Crap, what's up?" he repeated.

"New day, new life pending, one without someone I have been with for a long long time."

"So, what are your plans?"

"I just don't know Andy" she replied exposing seeds of doubt in her decision.

"Okay, let's look at the situation, Brian is only a suspect at the moment, his name is not public, yet."

"You have had time to think about things, do you want to leave him? you have had time to think of the past and all you were involved in, is there anything you want to tell me about what you guys got up to and who with?"

"No" Replied Sandra quickly.

"Okay, do me a favour, if you are going to wander around here in your dressing gown make sure it is properly fitted and tied," he said

"Sorry," she said sheepishly pulling closed her attire.

As they sat across the table from each other Andy stared into Sandra's eyes as she tried to avert her gaze from his. Andy knew deep down that she was hiding something from him and probably her daughter Susan. Andy was clock watching as he knew she had to get back to the east end and face Brian.

"Tell you what Sandra I am going to get a shave and a shower you have that time to think about it"

"Think about what?"

"What you are going to tell me," he said leaving the table and going into the bathroom locking the door behind himself.

After his shower and dressed ready to make his way to the east end, Andy went back into the living room and saw that Sandra had barely moved, she was still sitting at the table wearing only her dressing gown and staring into the empty cup in front of her.

"Well?" said Andy annoyed that she was not dressed ready to leave the flat.

"Sit down," she said staring out the window and pointing at the seat next to her.

Over the following thirty minutes, Sandra poured out her heart to Andy, about her life with Brian, as she did before but this time, she went into depth about the who and where over the past few years. What was expected of her and a few other wives who had become wrapped up in what was probably one of the most depraved and sordid scenes of the late seventies, early eighties, and she confessed that she was terrified if it ever reached court, and the full extent of everything becoming public knowledge. She said that it was only wives that could be present at Games Nights never girlfriends or outsiders.

"Andy, you do know nothing will ever come of this?"

"Meaning what exactly?" he replied looking into her eyes.

"This goes too high" she replied.

"So, what about the kids involved in all this?"

"They were and are expendable, in care and nobody cares about them, just toys for us"

"You also?" He asked.

"No Reply Andy" she replied looking away averting her eyes from his then rising from the table and making her way into the bedroom to get dressed for their journey to her home, and Brian.

Andy drove out to the east end and stopped outside the Berger house. Sandra leaned over and kissed Andy on the cheek. He took hold of her hand with his.

"Make the right decision Sandra, here is the phone number for Ricky's call me when you are ready."

"Thank you," she said as she got out of the car.

Andy watched as she went up the pathway a forlorn figure.

"Hiya," said Andy cheerfully as the door opened to his brother's house.

"Come in," said Ricky as Andy followed him into the large kitchen.

"Hey Andy," said Alice in a quiet voice barely glancing at him as she wiped the surfaces of the large kitchen worktops.

"Would you like a drink?" Ricky said rattling a glass with ice in it in front of Andy's face.

"Tea, straight, no ice" replied Andy flashing a glance at Alice as Ricky poured a large whisky.

"Hey, man is it not a bit early for that?"

"Never too early for a fine Scotch," he said slurring his words

"If you say so," said Andy with his back leaning against a worktop with his hands deep in his trouser pockets and shoulders hunched.

"I am going to the lounge, let you two talk about me."

"Ricky man what is going on?" Andy asked in a raised voice as his brother made his way back to the lounge.

"What is going on is, I am finished, not even my mates will give me a job, so all this has to go, our mum will have to go into a care home, god only knows what is going to happen to Alice and the kids now, oh the jungle drums are beating you are in the shit also and you were central to the downfall of some important people, you and some guy called Bobby."

"Where did all this come from?" Andy enquired flashing a look at Alice who looked in his direction nodding her head.

"Where do you think? you are not one of us, never will be."

"Hey, how is my mate doing at your office," said Ricky leaning against the hallway wall taking a swig from the glass of whisky.

"Ricky, who is your mate at my office?" asked Andy pushing himself upright and walking over the doorway and facing Ricky.

"Ralph, Ralph McGrory have you met him yet?"

"No, is he a new cop?" replied Andy casually not giving anything away that he had already met him.

"Nah, he is your new Chief Superintendent."

"Oh well, wait until he meets me then," Andy said with a smile shaking his head.

"Oh, he is well aware of who you are Andy, trust me" replied Ricky looking at his brother and swirling the contents of his glass.

"What does that mean?"

"You and your pal Bobby, as I said, he is well aware of both of you Brian Berger saw to that," he said with venom in his tone

"What has he got to do with it?"

"Colleagues for years and brothers, get the message, Andy?"

"Oh right" replied Andy watching as Ricky went into the lounge slamming the door behind him.

Andy looked over at Alice and shook his head. She just stared at him. Alice looked tired and drawn as she leaned against the kitchen units behind her.

"What is going on Alice?" he asked with sadness in his voice

"Andy it has been like this for days, the alcohol has taken over from the gambling."

"Are you ok?"

"Honestly, Andy I can't do this anymore I am thinking of leaving here and taking the kids"

"Where would you go?"

"Back to my Mum and Dads they have spare rooms, I have been offered a job so money would be no problem when I get started.

"I would miss you and the kids," he said pausing, "but you have to do what is right for you and the kids they cannot live like this, in this atmosphere."

"Oh, you would get to see them, Andy, no fear of that and me also."

"Okay, what about my mum."

"She is what has kept me here all this time to be truthful."

"Let me get that sorted please," he said worriedly.

"Fine thank you" as she wrapped her arms around him, and the door opened with Ricky having a clear view of the scene staggering into the kitchen.

"What is going on here?" he shouted.

"Nothing Ricky not what you are thinking right now."

"Yeah right" as he lifted the bottle of whisky returning to the lounge."

"Shit that was close," said Alice.

"What happened was a wonderful one-off situation Alice" whispered Andy holding her tightly as the telephone rang.

"Hello Alice, speaking, yes hold on please," she said.

"Andy this call is for you," said Alice.

He took the phone; it was Sandra asking Andy to pick her up immediately.

"Alice, I have to go I am sorry." He said grabbing his car keys from the worktop where he had laid them on his arrival.

"No problem."

"Say goodbye to Ricky for me."

"Sure."

They exchanged a quick kiss at the door looking into each other's eyes "Take care you" he said.

"Yes, I shall" she replied.

When he arrived at the Berger household he waited outside for Sandra to appear. Andy watched as the door opened and Sandra stepped outside carrying an additional bag and walking towards his car followed by Brian. Andy leaned over and opened the passengers' door from the inside to let Sandra in.

"Hello, Andy."

"Hello, Brian."

"Tell my protégé, McGrory, I am proud of him."

"I shall do, along with everything else I know, now close the door."

Brian slammed the car door closed striking Sandra's' arm in the process.

"Well that shall be the door closed are you okay?" he said trying to make light of the situation as she held her arm where it had been struck.

"Yes, hunky-dory" was all Sandra said as she looked out of the window at Brian who was standing on the path.

They set off along the street with its well-manicured gardens before heading for the motorway. Most of the journey was done in silence.

"You okay?" asked Andy as they stopped at a set of traffic lights.

"Yes great, free woman to do as I please with whom I please, even you."

"Doubt it, so here is the deal, you behave you can stay, misbehave you are gone."

"We shall see," said Sandra

"Tonight, we shall discuss this with Susan over dinner."

"You wouldn't" she replied looking at Andy in disbelief.

"Watch this space" he replied as the lights changed from red to green.

Sandra went so quiet over Andy's last comment and in the manner, it was said.

"Hey, babes how was your day?" asked Andy when Susan got home from the school.

"Great how was yours?"

"Hi mum, did everything go alright with dad?"

"Yes, dear we can sort things out amicably."

"That is good I am pleased."

"How did you two get on?" asked Susan.

"Well, Sandra?" said, Andy throwing her a glance awaiting her reply which unnerved her

"Yes, we got on fine and you will both be pleased to know dad is paying for rented accommodation."

"Meaning what?" asked Andy.

"I won't be here much longer."

"Well, mum you are welcome here as long as you want."

"Thank you, dear," said Sandra looking at Andy.

After dinner Andy said he was off to the gym and headed out on his own arriving in the car park a short time later, He needed the space to be alone and get back into training. With the car parked and bag uplifted from the rear seat, he recognised the red Audi parked near to the main entrance. The large rotating door beckoned and as he pushed it around a familiar lady stood on the other side of the glass door.

"Happy New Year Catherine."

"You also Andy."

"How are you?" he asked.

"Good thanks."

"And your sister and brother?" he inquired

"They are both fine thank you for asking."

"That's good I am happy for you."

"Thank You," said Catherine.

The meeting seemed strained as they had not seen each other for some considerable time and the interaction was somewhat muted. Their paths had not even crossed while Andy was on his secondment.

"I heard your news that you were engaged now, congratulations," said Catherine.

"Thank you."

"She is a very lucky lady," said Catherine her eyes looking downwards.

"Are you seeing anyone, Catherine?" inquired Andy.

"No, not seen anyone since we parted company."

"How is your Barry.?"

We are still in the same house, doing the same things, and he will never change."

"Catherine, I want to say something to you."

"Okay,"

"I loved you and I mean loved you, probably the first woman I have ever loved."

"And, me you Andy, still do see ya, Andy," she said as she left the building carrying her kit bag desperate to end the conversation.

Andy watched as she went to her car and opened the drivers' door throwing her bag into the back seat. As Catherine was about to get into her car she looked up and saw Andy standing under the lights of the reception area watching her. Her heart was in pieces and she knew his was also even though he was with Susan, Catherine would forever be in his heart.

In the gym, Andy vented his frustrations out on everything he could as the sweat poured down him. As was his habit he ventured into the sauna where a calmness came over him before returning to the flat.

"Oh, Susan your man looks fit tonight," said Sandra.

"Mum" she replied in a tone of disapproval.

"Thank you, Sandra," said Andy followed by "That was what you were saying today also, wasn't it?"

Sandra was aghast at this comment as she did not think he would say anything in front of Susan.

"Well not quite" she replied.

"Meaning?" As he flashed a look at her.

"Well I was just saying how handsome you were, and my daughter was lucky to have you."

"Ah, right my misunderstanding Sandra sorry."

"No problem" she replied staring at him as he walked away.

"Oh, mum you are going to get yourself into trouble if you keep this up," said Susan.

"Oh, goodie" replied Sandra.

As Susan crawled into bed with Andy, he suggested that it might be a good idea if Sandra found a place of her own as soon as possible and Susan agreed saying that after years living with someone, she would have to get used to the idea of living alone.

Andy then updated Susan about Ricky and Alice, his alcohol intake, and the rift it was causing with Alice. He told her he was worried about his mum having to go into a care home for the elderly with the possibility of Alice returning to her parents' house with the kids.

"We don't have our troubles to seek at the moment Andy that is for sure," said Susan.

"No, we sure don't, and we don't need any more to contend with" was his reply as they snuggled in together comforting one another.

Andy and Susan rose at the same time the following morning and he saw her off to school. He got dressed and went to the gym for an early morning session in the swimming pool before the schoolkids arrived for their free lessons. Dried and back in his loose white top, jogging pants, and trainers he went back to the car and drove to the flat. He was dreading going back to his place as he knew Sandra would get up to her tricks again.

He went into the living room and threw his bag onto the couch and switched on the coffee percolator.

"Hello Andy," said Brian.

"What are you doing in here?" He enquired spinning on his heels to look at Brian standing behind him.

"I've come to take Sandra home she called me earlier to come and get her."

Andy saw Sandra come into the room behind Brian "Is this true Sandra?"

She hesitated in her reply "He needs me, Andy."

"Yeah I am sure he does Sandra, does Susan know about this arrangement."

"No" replied Sandra.

"Why do I get a gut feeling something is not quite right here Sandra?"

"This has nothing to do with you," said Brian.

"Since when did you change your name to Sandra?" said Andy with the deadly stare only he could muster to put the fear of death into someone.

"Tell you what, this is my flat Brian, I would be obliged if you would go and wait in the car."

Brian turned and stared at Sandra and she nodded at him to go to the car. Brian left the flat and went downstairs. Andy looked out of the window and saw Brian get into the driver's seat of his car.

"What has changed Sandra?"

"I can't go through with all this Andy, all this unrest between us and having to start again."

"So, you are going back and put up with his needs and wants.?"

"Yes, Andy has to be that way."

"Sandra, what if he is rounded up and charged then has to go to jail?"

"Well, I get the house and the money to myself while he is away."

"Geezuz, what an outlook on life Sandra," he said softly shaking his head.

"Bonus is I will get to see more of Sheena now bye Andy and thank you."

Lifting her case, she made her way to the door telling Andy to look after their daughter as it would be unlikely that he would be allowed back in their house. She also asked Andy to tell Susan to call her when she got home from school and she would try and explain her reasons for returning home to Brian. Sandra closed the door behind her on the way out. Andy watched as she put her case into the boot of the car then got in the front passengers' seat. The Berger car pulled slowly out of the street and back towards the east end of the city.

For the rest of the day, Andy pottered about the house cleaning and tidying up, changing the sheets on the spare bed vacated by Sandra, and washing them.

"Hi babes I am home" was the familiar cry from Susan as she waltzed into the living room.

"Where is mum?"

"Hi, you seem in a good mood today was it a good one."

"Yes, great day today, everything went well, you haven't said where mum is."

"She has gone."

"Gone?"

"She has gone home Susan, back to your dad."

Susan sat down speechless on the couch, arms folded in front of her shaking her head from side to side, almost in disbelief after everything that happened. Andy told her about the events after he got back from the gym and them leaving together.

"My dad was here?" She went silent and paused, "Okay, you cannot be serious, right?"

"Nope, your mum wants you to call her now that you are home."

"I can't, I just can't, not right now, I need time to think about this, something not right Andy."

"That is what I said but she said to me it is what she has to do."

"No, no, no Andy something is bubbling under I can feel it" as she got up and paced the floor.

After a few hours and dinner with Andy, they sat curled up on their couch discussing what may or may not have changed Sandra's mind to go home. Andy suggested that the only way to find out what was going on was to phone her mum and try and get the truth from her. Susan sat there silently contemplating her next move. She moved slowly from the couch and towards the phone resting her hand on the receiver and looking at Andy. Andy could hear the dialling tone when Susan began to dial the number to her former home. Susan listened to the ringing tone at the opposite end of the line.

"Hello?" said Sandra.

"Hello, mum."

"Hello Susan, it is so good to hear your voice again."

"Mum, what is going on?"

The conversation was one way, Susan listened to her mum. Andy noticed that she had tears in her eyes, and they began to trickle down her cheeks one at a time. Susan was a hardy soul who had come through the incident at the school a few weeks earlier without fear but something different was happening this time.

"Mum, I will always be there for you no matter what happens, and this door will always be open."

Susan hung up the phone and collapsed onto the settee and into Andy's arms in a flood of tears and she cried like a baby, something Andy had never experienced from Susan before. All Andy could do was to hold her close at this time.

"Thank you," said Susan.

"For what?"

"Everything, mum is, em, staying there for now," she said.

"Okay, if that is what she wants to do there is nothing we can do Susan."

"I know, but there is something wrong about this whole scenario she said that you are about to find out about everything whatever that means" Susan paused for thought. "Oh no, please God no," she said, "please, not Kerry of all people."

Andy got a bad feeling about what was about to come from Kerry if she appeared after her shift.

Wednesday night Andy reported for duty early and looked through the reports for the past few days.

"Hiya Andy," said a familiar voice as she wrapped her arms around his neck in a soft friendly chokehold.

"Hiya June so glad you are here," he said patting her forearm

"Now why would you need me, Andy?" she asked.

"Because I trust you so much, especially for this one."

"What have you got this time?"

Andy sat and told June everything about the enquiry he had been involved in, who was involved and allegedly involved, the connections they had in the force and outwith, he did not want her to be compromised in any way.

"Geezuz Andy when you go for something you go for it big style."

"I am giving you the chance to walk away June."

"Like you, I don't do walk-away."

"June, I haven't a clue what is going to happen tonight."

"Okay, let's do it then."

DS Anderson and the rest of the crew entered the room, Danny looked at June.

"Keep him on a short leash"

"No problem Danny."

"Right Mr Blackmore, he are the rules, you make a mess of this whatever you are going to do, and you are gone, is that understood?"

"Yes Sergeant, the thing is I don't know what is going to happen tonight," he said looking at June.

"Well, good luck I hope this is all worthwhile"

"Thank you, Sergeant," replied Andy lifting a set of car keys and leaving the office followed by June

Just before seven o'clock, Andy pulled the unmarked car up near to the arranged meeting point switching off the engine and getting comfortable.

"Tell me something Andy, I get the impression I know more about what may happen here tonight than Liam Anderson does?"

"All anyone needs to know at the moment is half of what you know June" at which point he saw someone walking down the road towards them. Andy confirmed to June that it was Kerry Ferguson.

Kerry got into the rear seat of the police car and Andy drove to a quiet secluded area nearby. Kerry was silent until the car stopped.

"Andy, who is she?"

"This is June a colleague of mine."

"Andy this was not the deal."

"Kerry there was no deal other than nothing would be recorded in writing other than notes."

"Kerry, I trust June with my life, and I would not set you up that is a promise."

Kerry sat looking at June as if weighing her up.

"You double-cross me, and you will regret it, Andy Blackmore. Remember, if you were not with Susan you would be getting none of this"

"Andy you are not going to like what I am going to tell you guys because you will know some people involved and you will never get me into a court."

"Thank you for being so honest Kerry." Said June in a soft reassuring tone.

"This is my parting gift before university and a new life, for you guys to stop what is going on."

Kerry looked at Andy and June then began her story.

"When I was about six or seven, I was taken into care, I never knew who my father was, my mother could not cope and turned to drink, there were different "uncles" in the house almost every night. The Social Work Department was involved for as long as I can remember, and I was taken into care. While I was in the home, I got told my mother had died. So, I was on my own. After primary school, I went to Bankvale and I knew I was good at school and decided even at that age I could make something of myself and I was encouraged by my teachers to do as best as I could. I watched others fall around me into a life of drink and drugs, the boys and the girls, life was a joke to them. I kept myself to myself and in the home, I could hear them going in and out of each other's rooms but if the night shift could sit and watch the telly nobody bothered about what was happening upstairs. I met a guy when I was going on for fourteen at the school and he told me he had a friend who could get us a lot of money, so I was interested, and he said it was at a games night. When I asked what type of games, he said I could go with him and see for myself and I didn't need to play any games if I didn't want to. So, I thought what's the harm in a game's night, but I soon found out. We got picked up and taken to a house, a big house, there was a lot of men there and a few women" We got some alcohol supplied to us I refused the drugs, a white powder it was, then I met an older man who asked if I was a virgin which I was then and that night I went back to the home with five hundred pounds in my pocket. For the first few months, I was picking up a lot of money one party a week. Nobody questioned where I was getting the money because I kept a little for myself and I stashed the rest in a secret place. Then as time went by, I got to know who the men and the women were at the parties. Some were councillors and businessmen; some were police officers some were their guests just out for the evening. It wasn't just young girls that were at the party, there were guys there as well, they were there for the guys who liked younger boys and then there were the women who liked younger boys also, they were known as the "virgin takers" they got the boys aroused then had them in front of everyone who wanted to watch. This went on for a few of years, it was easy you just said to staff you were going out with your pals, go to the party house or club, get changed into your work clothes, school uniforms, nurses outfits whatever they were paying for that night so that was the game, doctors and nurses, teachers and pupils whatever doesn't matter but it is still going on and I want it to stop that is where you come in Jeanna and Angelina and a few others are involved as young as twelve now. Your Susan was a godsend to me Andy and she got me through the latter part of my final year at school when she came in as the Deputy Headteacher. When we met in the pub it was great to see her again. Andy, when she came in with her mother I went into a state of shock, to be honest, I knew who she was, she was one of the "virgin takers" along with a pal of hers who was younger. Her husband, who would be Susan's dad was a regular of mine, I made a lot of money from him and a few of his mates, not all were cops to be fair, some had fairly good jobs, some were professional people, all were nothing more than dirty scumbag perverts. I can tell you and I am going, to be honest, I kept a diary on them all, names, occupations, married or single, ages of the boys or girls they liked, what their preferences were sexually, times and places we met I have a full history, Andy. I was going to get revenge for everything they put me and the others through when we were so vulnerable and needed to be loved, not abused by them and their rich friends, I was going to destroy them all and drain them of every penny they had. You know Andy you have renewed my faith in guys because you have sat there and listened to me, you also June and I thank you for that, you have been non-judgemental as far as I can tell. I can see why Andy asked you here June and although he is with Susan you two are good together. Andy, I could fancy the pants off you if circumstances were so different, but they are not. Maybe someday in the future people will believe us and listen to me, Jeanna and Angelina and everyone else but the way the system is just now we shall not be believed. This is my parting gift to you Andy Blackmore and I want June by your side throughout this enquiry and Susan by your side for a long time" as she handed him a sealed brown envelope and alighted from the car ready to continue her journey to St Andrew's University and a new life.

Andy and June watched as Kerry disappeared into the darkness of the night. Andy wondered if he would ever see or hear from Kerry Ferguson again.

Andy looked at June, tears were streaming down her face, she was choked with emotion and little if anything was said. Andy looked down at the sealed brown envelope feeling the contents and knew he was now in possession of the diary that could bring down so many.

June opened the door of the car and went to the rear of the vehicle where she was violently sick until there was nothing left in her stomach. "Oh, Christ Andy this whole system, us, everyone, has failed those kids."

"Yes," he replied.

"Andy, I need a favour mate."

"Anything for you."

"Take me to Sheena's house please I will direct you."

"June?"

"Please do it, something I need to know."

"Okay,"

Andy pulled up outside Sheena's semi-detached house in a quiet street on the outskirts of Glasgow.

"June are you sure about this."

"We are finished Andy I have to put this to bed tonight."

Andy sat in the car as he watched June go into Sheena's house and close the door behind her. He could see June walking around the living room through the partially open Venetian blinds, her arms raised and remonstrating. When she left the house after about ten minutes, she slammed the door so hard she almost took it off its hinges.

"Drive Andy and drive now" she shouted.

"Can I ask something please tell me you did not hit her?" he said calmly.

"No, now drive," said a raging June demanding he drove away.

Andy headed for the office in silence as a furious June sat beside him.

"Right back to where we spoke to Kerry."

"Why."

"Just do it man" she shouted thumping the dashboard with her fists

Andy pulled up at the spot they had interviewed Kerry, which was isolated, June got out of the car leaving the door open and screamed a piercing scream that filled the night air before crying hysterically. Andy put his head on the steering wheel with his eyes closed knowing what had been revealed at Sheena's without opening the envelope.

Andy got out of the car and sat against the bonnet. The doors were open on both sides and the small interior light illuminating the inside of the vehicle. June slowly walked back towards Andy who held out his arms and embraced her as she sobbed uncontrollably.

"I am so sorry June," he said.

"If I had known where this was going, I would never have brought you here tonight" he continued

"I know Andy it is not your fault" she replied

"Do you know what hurts most everything I had with her was a lie," she said sobbing and trying to control her emotions.

"There is something I need to ask you and I want the truth, Andy."

"Okay,"

"Over Christmas or New Year did you know she was seeing Sandra Berger?"

"Yes June, I did."

"Thank You for the truth" as she wiped her eyes.

"We can't go back to the office looking like this mate," she said.

"Oh, I know let's find a late-night garage get a cup of tea."

"Yeah, good idea."

"Then we have to talk seriously."

"Envelope and contents?"

"Yes."

"Whose turn is it for the tea then," said Andy putting June into a playful headlock.

"Yours for getting me into this mess" she replied grabbing his forearm.

"Andy Blackmore, I love you like the best partner I have ever had in this job."

"Well June I love you too as the best female partner I have had since I started."

"Andy I am the only female partner you have had since you started."

"Well, that says it all then," he said laughing as they got back into the car.

Andy knew the local garage would be open and he pulled the car onto the forecourt. "Milk and sugar as usual" he enquired. "One sugar only I am cutting back," said June. She watched as he went to the machine under the strong fluorescent lights in the garage shop then chatting to the lady at the pay desk who she saw giggling.

"Geez you love to flirt," said June, "Yeah hence the reason half price" as he handed the cups to June with the lids tightly closed and driving from the forecourt to a dark location nearby.

As they sat in the car overlooking a loch where the light of the moon reflected off the water they sipped on their teas. The brown envelope lay on the dashboard unopened, Andy and June sat in silence. In his rear-view mirror, Andy saw the lights of a slow-moving vehicle approaching. He took the envelope from the dashboard and stuffed it down the back of his jeans.

The vehicle stopped behind them. Andy stepped out the car leaving the door open to be confronted by Chief Superintendent McGrory and another male unknown to him. "Good evening sir" June heard him say.

"Blackmore isn't it?"

"Yes, sir."

"Who is the female in the car with you?"

"This is Constable June Brown sir she works in Bankvale."

"Good evening June." He said leaning on the roof and bending forward and looking into the car.

"June, this is Chief Superintendent McGrory our new Divisional Commander."

"Good evening sir," she replied.

"Can I ask why you are both sitting here in the darkness overlooking the loch."

"We were on an enquiry sir and we managed to grab a cup of tea."

"What enquiry?"

"Housebreakers sir and also a pile of vandalisms' happening nearby in isolated premises sir."

"Ah right" was his reply but dubious about the answer he was given.

Andy watched as the unknown male walked around the police vehicle with his torch lit and looking into the vehicle as if looking for something or someone.

"Is your pal looking for something sir?"

McGrory looked at Andy "Maybe" was his reply.

"Well I can help him if he wants, that is if he is a police officer."

"Oh, he is, believe me, he is."

"Hey, pal can I help you?" Andy said as June cringed.

"No thank you," said the male politely as he looked at McGrory shaking his head in the negative.

"Good luck with your enquiry Blackmore nice to meet you, Constable Brown."

"You also sir" she replied as McGrory and his companion went back to their vehicle.

Andy and June watched as the vehicle drove off into the darkness. Andy got back into their vehicle and June saw Andy puff out his cheeks letting out a long breath, clenching the steering wheel.

"What was that all about," asked June?

"That was all about, what could be in this," said Andy reaching behind himself and pulling the envelope out of the back of his jeans

"Andy what is going on here mate, what is inside that envelope?"

"June, you and I are the only two people besides Kerry that knows this exists."

"So, what were they looking for?"

"June, I think they were looking for Kerry" he replied staring at the envelope.

"Oh my god, surely not."

"Just a feeling June, just a feeling"

"Who knew about tonight, Andy?"

"DS Anderson."

"Anybody else?"

"I have not got a clue, I asked him to have you here tonight, I don't know if he told anyone."

"June I am way out of my depth pal, what am I going to do with this envelope?"

"Well certainly not lodge it as a production, you will never see it again, so if I was you take it home, Kerry gave it to you to take care of."

"She gave it to us June, you heard what she said also, so it is us now."

"I don't know if I can handle this Andy, this is massive."

"Okay, I am having a thoughtful moment," he said.

"Geez, I hate your thoughtful moments."

"Come to the flat when we finish, stay the night and tomorrow we open the envelope together."

"Oh yeah, me you and Susan in bed together that'll be a surprise for her in the morning."

"Noooooooo spare box room for you, are you up for it?"

"Yeah, why not, if that is Okay with Susan?"

"I shall take care of things there," said Andy.

Andy completed his shift report in the late shift section for the morning briefing. "Enquiries made re housebreakings and vandalism. Some success but nothing further to report" signed AB.

As Andy and June walked to their respective cars, a hand turned the page of the evening report which was relayed by telephone to the Divisional Commander.

"June go to my flat wait until I get there," said Andy.

"Why to make sure you are not being followed park in the street near to mine."

"Okay," she responded.

Andy watched as June left the police car park, nothing moved at her back. Andy left the car park a short time thereafter. He immediately saw a car at his back. He drove into his street and parked up hoping June was nearby and watching from a safe distance.

Andy watched as the car extinguished its headlights as he went into his close. Andy being Andy opened the back door to the close, cut through the backcourts and came around behind the vehicle that had been followed him to his flat. Quickly and silently like a commando, he was on the pavement opening the car door, dragging the driver out of his seat pinning him to the ground watched by June who by now was in the horrors as to who the driver may be.

"How can I help you?" asked Andy

"I am here to look after you, you asshole," said the man struggling to speak

"Well, you are not making a good job of it are you?"

"Who sent you?"

"Anderson, DS Anderson"

"Why?"

"Because he wants you kept safe, you are going to break my arm"

"No mate, I could have done that a while ago, now get back on your car and go, I don't need you"

Andy watched as the car drove off and June appeared out the darkness. They went up to the flat together out with the gaze of a minder sent to look after him or even, both. They crept into the flat not to waken Susan. Andy showed June where she could sleep for the night. Andy slipped gently into bed with Susan, she only moved briefly to wrap her arm around him.

As Andy lay there with Susan wrapped around him, he thought of what secrets lay inside the envelope and what devastating revelations may influence their relationship and his working relationship with June. Why was DS Anderson so interested in his safety, now that was something he had to clear up and quickly and just who was a threat….

Chapter Eight

S usan was first up in the morning and returned to the bedroom straight from the living room. She shook Andy awake
"Andy, whose boots are those in the living room?"

"June's"

"Why is she here?"

"I shall tell you everything later she is in the spare room."

"She better stay there then, or you are going to need some serious surgery" she replied.

"Promise I will speak to you later it is too early to get into everything."

"Good job I trust you" she replied.

"Kiss?" he asked.

"I shall see you for a little while tonight when I get in before you go to work," said Susan.

"Okay, Love you."

Susan alighted from the close and as she went to her car, she saw a car parked opposite the flat with a male in the driver's seat. The male occupant appeared to be watching her. "That's unusual," she thought to herself. She drove to the school and phoned Andy immediately upon her arrival from her office telephone.

Andy stirred from his sleep and answered the phone.

"Hi."

"Andy it is me look out of the window, Ford Granada, blue, a guy in the driver's seat is it still there?"

"Yeah," he said looking down onto the vehicle.

"Is the guy still in it."

"Yep."

"Right he was watching me when I left the flat and getting into my car."

"Okay, leave it with me, and say nothing to anyone please."

Andy went to the spare room and chapped on the door. "June, we have a problem," he said, and he told her the situation and that he wanted her to stay in the flat as he was going to the gym and to see if the car would follow him out of the street. He told her to leave and go home if the car followed him.

Gym bag in hand Andy went to his car. As he pulled out of the street June watched the Ford Granada leave also. She gathered her belongings and was about to leave the flat to go home when the phone rang and went straight to the answering machine. "Andy this is Sandra, what have you done? I have had Sheena on the phone, she had a massive row with June last night you have to call me," she said as the line went dead. June was tempted to pick up the phone during the call but resisted before driving home with the words of Sandra Berger ringing in her ears.

After an hour Andy left the gym, but rather than going home he drove directly to the office and into the car park. The vehicle that was following him did not follow him. Andy went straight to DS Anderson's office knocked on the door and marched straight in without waiting for an invite.

"Sergeant would you like to tell me what is going on and why you are having me followed."

"Sorry I have a visitor I shall call you back," said DS Anderson replacing the receiver on the cradle.

As he folded his arms and leaned back in his seat he said.

"Nice to see you, Andrew, sit down, please. What do you want to know?"

"The truth would be good," said Andy "who were the guys you left the office with?" this time Andy was calm and polite towards DS Anderson.

"They were two surveillance officers who came to update me on an enquiry."

"Can you say what enquiry?" he asked.

"Yes, certainly, the one you were, or are, involved in."

"So, Bobby and I were watching the children's home and they were watching who? us?"

"No, they were watching the suspects in this case along with a big team of surveillance officers."

"Sergeant Bobby and I saw you with Brian Berger go into the Valentino Club together."

"Yes, I knew Brain Berger years ago, he was my target and I persuaded him to introduce me into the Games Nights at the club hence the reason I was with him. I must admit you nearly blew it when I saw you leaving there."

"Did you say to anyone I was seeing Kerry last night or say anything in front of anyone."

"No Andy I spoke to June personally and told her to phone in sick and come straight here to meet you so there was no third party involved."

"Do you have any idea why the Divisional Commander happened to be out late last night accompanied by someone he claimed to be a police officer and happened to find June and I down by the side of the loch, having a cup of tea I may add, and the male taking great interest in our car?"

"Now that is something, I know nothing about other than he was Berger's boy."

"I am barely in the door and all this is going on around me, I don't understand why this is happening to me, to be honest, but, what I do know is that we have a leak somewhere who is feeding the new boss with information, and I am worried for Susan and everyone else connected to me, how the hell did he know where we were last night that is the question?"

"Andy, I do not know" replied DS Anderson.

"Okay, two more questions before I go. One, why was there a 'goon' sent by you to look after me and two who is the guy in the Granada following me this morning."

"Okay, the truth is the 'goon' you refer to was and is there to look after you and Susan as we have information certain people are out to get you for the work you have done and exposing high ranking officials. Secondly, you scared the shit out of him and the guy in the Granada is there to do the same job."

"Since I came to this department DI O'Dowd seems to have been missing, where is he?"

"Seconded is the only answer you are going to get to that."

"Can you do me a favour please apologise to the guy I scared the shit out of."

"Yes, certainly I can, but do it yourself," said DS Anderson as the door opened.

Andy looked around, instantly recognising the driver of the car, "Hey mate, I am sorry" as he stood up and raised his hand and shook his minders hand. "I don't think we got off to a good start, forget about me make sure Susan is okay, please"

"Yeah sure that is under control as we speak," said the plainclothes officer "That matter is well in hand" he replied.

Looking at both of his colleagues Andy shook his head "I need to get my head around all of this" As Andy reached for the door handle, he stopped and turned around. I want to thank both of you for your honesty so one last question "Why choose me when you have got more experienced officers here?"

DS Anderson looked at the unnamed undercover officer before he said anything. He got the nod.

"Andy sit please for a moment," asked DS Anderson "we, in the CID, have had our eye on you for a while for a secondment. We learned that you were in a relationship with Susan Berger who happened to be the daughter of Brian and Sandra Berger who were already in the sights of a special unit which had been put together to investigate the abuse of children in care. They had hoped that you might get an insight into the Berger family and secret friends they may have or had but they got word back that you and Berger were at odds with each other."

Andy sat there listening intently.

The DS continued, "What did not help, was the fact that June was in a relationship with Sheena Gough who is in a relationship with Sandra Berger so when you asked for June to be with you we had deep reservations as to bringing June on board but as luck would have it she had a blazing row with her former girlfriend last night so Sheena Gough is now in the frame as part of the ring.

Andy said nothing but DS Anderson and the unnamed officer could see him thinking it was so obvious as he was staring into oblivion

"Wait a minute," then pausing "just hold on a minute that happened just over twelve hours ago. Did you bug the car I was using?" asked Andy.

He got no reply.

"Sheena Gough is being interviewed as we speak Andy," said the DS.

"You never answered my question" was Andy's' rapid reply with a stare to his DS.

"The answer is no we have our ways other than that."

Andy stood up and shook his head, once more heading towards the office door, looking towards DS Anderson and the plain-clothed officer he raised his right hand "Guys I have had it for the moment."

They recognised the strain he was under "Take your time young man" said 'the plainer.'

"Okay," said Andy as he left the office.

"You have a cracker there, give him time I may want him with me and us," said the officer.

"Yes, I know, keep him safe please," said the DS.

Andy left the office not completely satisfied with what he had heard. He didn't have a clue what to tell Susan as this went a lot deeper than what he ever imagined. The one thing that he was happy with was, neither mentioned the brown envelope handed over by Kerry.

Andy saw the answering machine indicating that he had one new message. Pressing play, he heard Sandra's voice and listened to the message about Sheena. He deleted it without calling back. Instead, he lay on the couch for a nap before Susan got home and the return to the streets with Bobby.

"Andy," said Susan shaking his shoulder awakening him from light sleep, "I have to ask you something that has been getting at me all day."

"Geez sorry I must have dozed off."

"Andy are you having an affair with June?" asked Susan.

"No, I am not" as he burst out laughing.

"Okay, I fail to find the funny side of that question I am being serious."

"Susan, June is a lesbian well, was a lesbian, whatever, up to recently she was with Sheena Gough."

"Are you winding me up?" she asked with a stunned look on her face.

"No, I am not I am being serious."

"How long have you known?" She asked getting annoyed.

"A while."

"And you said nothing?"

"Susan that is her private life nothing to do with me or us."

"But?" she stuttered.

"But nothing Susan."

"So why were you out with her last night, she should have been on your shift?"

"Because I asked for her to be with me, I did not want to speak to Kerry Ferguson alone, so I asked for June to be with me."

"Why did June not go home after that?"

"Because" he replied.

"Because is not an answer Andy" as he sensed anger in Susan's voice.

He also sensed this conversation was not going well.

"Because I don't trust anyone at the office, or in the office just now so we had to speak away from the office and as we were together last night I thought this would be the best place to discuss things this morning but I have made an error with that thought."

"What about Kerry is she Okay?"

"Yes, as far as I know, she is fine, she is so lovely and worships you."

"I just hope she gets away to Uni."

"What does that mean?"

"I hope everything that has happened does not stop her from being special."

"I agree," he said as he rose from the couch and looking at his watch.

"Time I was away lovely lady"

"Yeah, I know I don't like this shift," said Susan.

"It's only once a month for a few months," said Andy as he kissed Susan before leaving the flat.

As Andy walked into the office Bobby was there and asked how he got on being on his own for an evening. Andy advised him it was an eventful evening to which Bobby laughed saying that he had seen the late shift report of investigating housebreakings and vandalisms. Bobby and Andy discussed their plans for the evening. Andy had no crime reports left for him, Bobby had a few loose ends to pick up and to write off his reports.

Just before midnight, the control room Sergeant walked into the office.

"Uh Oh, Andy here comes the sniffer," said Bobby with a nod of the head and a chuckle.

"Bobby remember I am a Sergeant please."

"Here comes Sergeant Sniffer," said Bobby laughing.

"That is better."

"How are you doing Graham?"

"Nightshift bored as usual."

"Sergeant Graham Arnold this is Andy Blackmore ADC."

"Pleased to meet you, Sergeant."

"You too Andy" he replied.

Andy sat completing his paperwork while the Sergeant and Bobby chatted away and sipped on tea Andy had made them.

"Christ, Bobby guess who was in here last night?"

"Okay, give up," said Bobby."

"None other than Detective Chief Superintendent Willie Arnold down from Force Headquarters."

"Do you know he was in his ragtag and bobtail outfit like being on a mission" he continued.

"What was he doing here Graham?"

"Dunno he went out with the new guy, the new Chief Super."

"Andy," said Sgt Arnold.

"Yes Sergeant."

"Are you fairly new here?"

"Yes, suppose so" was his reply.

"You were on late last night did you see the DCS."

"Not sure I don't know that many bosses, especially from the FHQ" was his reply.

"Oh, you couldnae miss him six-foot-four brick shithouse of a man."

"Greying haired guy, black jacket, white casual shirt and denims?" asked Andy

"Yes, that is him," said Sergeant Arnold perking up.

"Nah never saw him."

"Eh? so how can you describe him so accurately?"

"Didn't know he was a DCS from FHQ saw him sucking the face off the new Chief Super."

"Where?" Asked the Sergeant with a renewed interest.

"At the back door."

"Really?" Said the Sergeant.

"Absolutely," said Andy.

"Gees wait until the troops know about this," he said leaving the office.

"Andy, Andy, Andy that will be around the shift by the time you finish your tea.," said Bobby

"Good" was his reply with a mischievous grin beaming across his face.

"Andy wandered about the office and into the control room."

"Sgt, I was joking about the DCS."

"Oh Okay," said Sergeant Arnold.

"The female civilian assistant turned and looked at Andy.

"Who are you?" she asked in a sexy sultry tone

"Andy" he replied politely.

"Andy who."

"Blackmore."

"Ah, so you are Blackmore."

"Well, the girls were right."

"Okay, enough I am engaged, playing the field days are over for me."

"Well Blackmore I am Jane, married, two kids and I want you big style."

Andy turned and left the control room.

"Thanks, Jane that sorted him out telling me lies," said Sergeant Arnold.

"You are welcome Graham" she laughed.

Bobby and Andy went out on patrol and carried out some enquiries that were pending but the evening drifted out to a quiet finish for both.

In the early hours of the morning, Andy left the office, he noticed that his minder was on his tail back to the flat where he parked up for the night. Somehow, he was going to have to tell Susan about the situation.

Andy got a few hours' sleep before heard the alarm on the clock go off to waken Susan for school. He waited until she was showered and had returned to the bedroom. Susan was surprised to see him awake and he told her that he would have to speak to her later when she got home. He did say that there would be a car at the close but just to ignore it and that it was a police vehicle.

When Susan left the flat Andy lay down for a few more hours sleep until he was rudely awakened by the phone ringing.

"Hello," Andy said lifting the receiver and rubbing his face trying to wake himself up a bit.

"Andy this is Sandra, you never called me back, I left a message for you."

"Sandra, so sorry, I was busy yesterday, how can I help you."

"I take it you know Sheena had been taken in by the police for questioning?"

"No Sandra I have nothing to do with all that now so I will not be party to any information."

"Andy you have caused a lot of trouble for a lot of people and they know that you are with Susan."

"I am sorry I don't understand," said Andy pretending to be confused, but fishing for information.

"Andy protect my daughter, our daughter."

"From whom Sandra?"

"People who want to harm you."

"Who wants to harm me? and can I ask you something how do you know all this?"

"I can't answer that now, but can we meet today?" she asked quietly.

"Yes sure, where?"

"The Book Shop, New City Road, midday?"

"Yes," he replied as he heard the phone at the opposite end of the line being hung up.

Andy knew, in Sandra, he either had a problem or a friend. Then there was his minder, do I lose him or let him tag along for the ride he thought. Andy left his flat and looked over at the vehicle parked nearby. He got into his car and drove to the local railway station where he parked up before going into the ticket office and purchasing a return ticket to the city centre. Looking around he noticed he was not alone on his platform or the one opposite as he was being watched closely. One was his minder the other was a mystery man.

The Book Shop on New City Road was a three-storey building with a coffee shop in the basement, it was a busy bookshop frequented by people from all walks of life due to its vast stock and diversity of books available.

"Hi," said the tall slim blonde female as she sat opposite Andy at the small table with two seats.

"Hi," said Andy as he looked up from a book, he had taken from one of the shelves.

He looked over her shoulder at his minder who was watching the proceedings. Andy saw him look at the female in a manner to suggest he had no idea who she was. Andy's minder rose from his table and made his way to the autobiography section. Andy excused himself from his table and returned his book to the shelf. His minder chooses a book named "The Honey Trap," with the subtitle, "The Downfall of a Politician". Andy got the message loud and clear as he went to the hobbies section where he loitered for a minute or two. "A Life in Photography" he chose and returned to the table.

"Are you a photographer?" Said his tablemate.

"No, but I have an interest in it."

"I am sorry I should have introduced myself I am Anika."

"Hi" he replied.

"You are?"

"I am...." he paused "here to meet the lady behind you, maybe another time?"

Anika looked behind her and seeing Sandra stared at her intently. They were known to each other, intimately.

"Yes, maybe another time, I would like that," said Anika as she left the table looking at Sandra.

He watched as Anika went to the upper floor which led to the exit.

"Hello Sandra, say nothing and follow my lead," he said to her as he kissed her cheek.

He went up the stairs holding Sandra's hand, confusing both Sandra and his minder. As he got to the upper floor, he noticed Anika browsing a section of books. Andy led Sandra from the store out onto the street where they sat on a public bench on the busy pedestrian precinct. She sat beside him. Andy watched the door to the bookstore and the lady who introduced herself as Anika exited and looked around.

"Sandra, who is she?"

"Who?"

"The blonde?"

"Anika Marina Pavlova" Sandra stared and went silent.

"Sandra?" said Andy trying to prompt her

"Anika is the Games Night organiser, I am ready to talk Andy," she said instantaneously

"What does that mean?"

"This has gone too far, take me to your office please."

"Why would she sit and speak to me, Sandra?"

"I think that you might find that Mr Berger may have something to do with this."

"Do you think she knows that I am a cop?"

"I don't know Andy to be honest, but I can't see him going that far, but who knows."

Andy knew that his back was covered as he walked with Sandra to the railway station and got the train out of the city and to his car. He took Sandra straight to his office and sat with her as DS Anderson and Danny prepared the relevant paperwork.

"Mrs. Berger are you here voluntarily?" asked DS Anderson

"Yes"

The voluntary attendance forms were completed and signed.

"Mrs. Berger do you wish the services of a lawyer"

"No"

"Can I ask why you are here?"

"I am going to make a full statement concerning your enquiry Sergeant I am going to tell all."

Andy went and sat in the office canteen drinking what seemed like gallons of tea as the hours rolled by. In the interview room, Sandra was revealing name after name of Senior Police Officers linked to her husband both current and retired, She revealed the names of local and national politicians who she knew were actively involved in the Games Nights. She revealed the names of senior social workers who were aware of the situation and although not involved in the actual Games Nights were getting paid to turn a "blind eye" to the time of night the girls were returning to the home, even falsifying records. She revealed that the whole operation was run with military precision to protect the players. She disclosed that most of the evenings were planned during secret meetings away from the public view and behind closed doors. Only four people would know the exact details of the next Games Night and where it was to take place. They, in turn, would pass the information onto others about an hour before the event. She admitted in full her involvement, implicating her husband, implicating her friend and lover Sheena Gough and many others in what would become a national scandal that would cost lives.

After approximately four hours of interviewing Sandra Berger, DS Anderson found Andy sitting in the canteen. DS Anderson looked exhausted by the stress and strain of the enquiry.

"Andy, never in my service have I taken a statement like that," he said putting on the kettle.

"Where is Sandra?" asked Andy.

"She is in the holding room."

"Can I see her?" he requested.

"Yeah why not I am going to have a coffee anyway."

"What are your plans for her Sergeant?"

"Do you know something, at this time I haven't a clue I have this huge statement, her admission to crimes and offences against kids, allegations against a lot of people of high esteem, I need to call the duty Procurators Fiscal to seek advice again. What shift are you meant to be?"

"six at night until two in the morning"

"It's after five now what about Susan?"

"She will be home now."

"Okay, take Sandra to her I will release her on standard Bail with special conditions."

"Come back here when you get things sorted, I will speak to Bobby tell him you will be in later."

With all the relevant paperwork sorted out concerning her release, Andy drove Sandra to his flat where she had to face Susan.

"Where have you two been?" asked Susan as they walked into the living room.

"I need to get ready for work, Susan you chat to your mum."

As he got changed into his work clothes having shaved and showered Andy could hear crying coming from the living room. He left the flat closing the door quietly hoping Susan would understand his silent exit.

Andy walked into the office where the small team he was part of was sitting chatting among themselves. That stopped immediately.

118

"Sorry mate," said Bobby looking at him.

"Can I make something clear here please?" said Andy as DS Anderson entered the office.

"See all this, the enquiry and, I know you are aware of what is going on, neither Susan nor I, are part of anything that has gone on. I have no doubt, knowing the way this job is this will follow me for years to come being connected to Brian and Sandra Berger through Susan. Think of the way she is feeling right now, they are her parents, Danny, Sergeant, I don't know what is in the statement she made to you guys today, we never discussed it on the way to my flat where she met up with her daughter. Right now I don't know where my Susan is, I left them together in the flat together, I don't know if she is still at the flat or with her mother or even what is happening, see being honest I don't care about me, I can go back to the sites but teaching is her life, all this could bring her career crashing down around about her"

As the office phone rang DS Anderson lifted the receiver. "Andy it is Susan for you," he said.

"I understand, I shall see you in the morning" they all heard him reply.

The team were looking at Andy "She is taking her mother home."

"Is that a good idea considering she has implicated her man?" asked DS Anderson.

"Well, she has to tell him that she was here first."

"Andy, do you honestly think he does not know she was here?" asked Bobby.

Andy placed his hands over his face as the reality of the situation dawned on him and the likelihood that Brian would know.

"McGrory" was the only word from Andy.

"Let's not jump to conclusions," said DS Anderson.

When Susan and her mother went into the family home, Brian Berger was standing waiting for them both. He had seen Susan's car draw up outside a few minutes earlier. With his legs splayed and clenched fists on his hips, his face was almost crimson with rage. He had been tipped off earlier that Sandra was at the police office from a reliable source of his.

"What have you done you, stupid stupid woman?" he screamed at Sandra.

"What I should have done years ago Brian."

"Dad, Mum, stop this please" pleaded Susan.

"Do you realise what that stupid cow has done to me, you, this family?"

"Let's calm down a minute dad," Susan said trying to remain as calm as possible under the circumstances standing between her parents

"Calm down? are you joking? or are you taking her side in all of this?" he shouted at Susan "It is your boyfriend that started all this. Do you think that I don't know that officers A and B that Burch referred to in his retirement press conference was Andy and his mate Bobby?" he asked staring at Susan.

Just then, the doorbell rang "Whoever that is get rid of them" he shouted as he watched Sandra go into the hallway. Sandra opened the door and placed her finger to her lips when she saw who was there. In silence, Sheena stepped into the hallway and placed her arms around Sandra hugging her tightly before walking into the living room.

"Great, this is all I need, you here," said Brian in a raised voice and an agitated state.

"She is here for me Brian, to be with me at this time, the time that I did what was right and will see you rot in jail in years to come," shouted Sandra.

"Listen," said Susan followed by a pause "I do not know the full extent of what you have all been up to, but what I do know is that I am proud of my Andy, so having said that I am going back down the road to the man I love, mum, our door is open to you at any time" as she turned to walk away.

"Susan," said Brian "wait, please," he asked in a soft voice as if pleading with her to stop.

"Why should I dad, you meant everything to me, you were the shining light in my life, so was mum, now, I just don't know, I need answers to everything before it is too late, I don't want you two to go to your graves and me asking myself, when,? where,? who,? what,? Do you understand dad?"

Susan and Sheena both watched Brian closely as he stood in the middle of the living room with his head bowed. The clenched fists had relaxed to open hands on his hips, his breathing was becoming gentler.

"I have an idea," said Sheena, calmly, "Why don't we get out of here and go for dinner somewhere, clear the air, and Susan, to put your mind at rest, we shall tell you everything, it will not be what you want to hear but you need to know," she said in a soft sympathetic tone

"Okay, I agree let's all go for dinner to a pub or somewhere please, clear the air, I will drive," said Brian.

Brian started the car, then suddenly he opened the door "Be right back, hang on" he said. He went into the house and made a phone call "Sorry about that just had to do something" he said as he got back into the car before setting off.

Bobby and Andy were going over Andy's reports for the PF, they could hear the sirens of emergency vehicles passing the office heading out of town. Bobby advised that Andy's reports overall were excellent, they tweaked little bits here and there to strengthen them up. Andy submitted the reports for typing.

The phone rang in the office and Andy knew it was an internal call by the ringtone.

"Andy its Amanda here in the control room, just to let you know a car has been driven off the pier at the Loch Restaurant and into the water"

"Thanks, Amanda"

"Bobby that was Amanda somebody has driven off the pier into the loch at the restaurant"

"What intentionally?"

"She never said." Replied Andy shrugging his shoulders.

"Okay, right we have nothing to do let's take a run down there see what is happening, just in case."

"Just in case what?" asked Andy.

"Just in case all is not right and we can see what the witnesses are saying, may just be an accident."

"Fine no problem, you drive?"

As Andy and Bobby reached the scene the place was filled with emergency vehicles, police officers from the Traffic Department were already present. Ambulances and the Fire Brigade were also standing by. Their engines were silent, but the blue lights filled the air as they rotated on their respective vehicles.

Andy looked around, it was his shift that was there, but he stood back letting them get on with their jobs. For once Andy was not part of this enquiry so he respected that as he watched his shift Sergeant, Geordie, Joe, and June interviewing witnesses to the incident.

"Sergeant, Bobby and I are here if you need a handout with statements."

"You are fine at the moment Andy wait in the car if we need you, we shall give you a shout" he replied as a crowd of people from the restaurant gathered around the area. It wasn't long before information started to emerge that there were bodies in the car lying on the floor of the loch. The only thing lighting up the night was the internal lights of the restaurant shining across the water from the massive windows and the reflection of the mass of blue lights.

Senior officers started to appear from all the services watched on by Bobby and Andy.

"Gaffers night out," said Bobby.

"Eh" was Andy's curious reply.

"Callouts for the bosses tonight treating this as a major incident for some reason" replied Bobby.

Andy saw June hovering about away from the throng of the officers in attendance.

"Hey pal," said Andy rolling down the window of the CID car.

"Hi Andy" she replied.

"What's going on?" he asked.

"There are two maybe three people in the car we don't think anyone got out" June informed Andy and Bobby

"That is sad," said Andy.

"Looks like deliberate by the driver, folk are saying he drove into the car park, turned and went straight off the pier at high speed, so the car is well into the loch, just have to wait on the underwater unit now"

"Do you have a make and registration number of the car June surely that will give us a place to start making enquiries"

"Most folks saw it from the side so there are conflicting reports about the registration number"

"June do you know Sheena was in for an interview."

"Yes."

"Do you know Sandra made a voluntary statement today?" said Andy.

"No, I didn't."

"Well, she did for over four hours."

"Geez, long haul" replied June.

"Yeah" he replied.

A police car arrived and out stepped the nightshift, police Superintendent. Bobby and Andy watched as he surveyed the scene then came over to the CID car.

"Who is Bobby."

"I am sir."

"Come with me" was the command.

"Yes sir" replied Bobby.

Bobby returned to the car "well that is it for us" he said. "They are treating this as a road accident cause unknown at the moment so that is it mate."

"Okay, good means we get to bed on time."

Before driving off Bobby looked around, "Andy, why the hell would the nightshift 'Super' come over to this car, ask for me, then tell me they are treating this as an accident?"

"Maybe he wanted to do something and justify being here."

As they headed back to the office the underwater unit vehicle passed in the opposite direction heading towards the loch.

Sitting in the office with the late-night radio playing away in the background the news came on at one o'clock. The headline report was the car in the loch. "Police have confirmed there are fatalities following a car entering the loch off the pier at the popular Loch Restaurant," said the newsreader.

"Did you hear that Bobby"

"Yeah, Andy do you want an early night, nothing doing here"

"You sure?" Andy asked "Yeah that would be great been here most of the day"

"Yeah on you go if I need you, I shall call you"

"Thanks, mate" replied Andy leaving the office

Andy opened the door to his flat quietly and went into the living room where he put the kettle on. He looked over and saw the answering machine indicating a message pending. As he raised his hand to press the play button, he thought to himself that the day had been long enough and decided it could wait. Andy got stripped in the living room and carried his clothes into the bedroom where he crawled into bed which he found to be empty. He put the bedside light on. Susan's side of the bed was empty. Looking at the clock it was far too late to phone her parents' house, so he assumed that she had stayed overnight with her mum. He thought that was probably the message on the answering machine that he chose to ignore until the morning as he drifted into a deep sleep.

The doorbell was ringing constantly so much so Andy wakened with a startled gaze into the dark room thinking he was dreaming rubbing his eyes and looking around himself. He crawled out of his bed and went to the door. He found June in floods of tears sobbing her heart out.

"June?"

"Answer your phone Andy for Christ sake."

"Eh, what do you mean, what are you doing here at this time of the morning."

"Andy the car in the loch, it's the Berger's Andy."

"June get in here."

"Okay, let's try this again," said Andy.

"Andy the car in the loch it's the Berger car."

"June who is or was in it please," said Andy panicking.

"Brian, Sandra, Sheena and Susan, Andy, Susan was in it, Susan was in the car" she sobbed.

As they went into the living room Andy went numb and collapsed onto the couch with June beside him their grief was inconsolable as they hugged tightly. Andy eventually got up and went to the answering machine.

"Hey Andy, its Brian Berger, remember I said you will never marry my daughter well believe me you asshole, tonight I am going to make sure you don't," said the voice from the dead.

"June, he killed them, he killed them all" stuttered Andy in disbelief at what he had heard.

3.30 am

As Andy and June comforted each other in their time of grief and loss there was a gentle tap at the door. Andy dragged himself off the couch and opened the door to find DI. O'Dowd and DS Anderson standing there. Just looking at him they knew Andy was aware of the situation. They went into the living room; they saw June sitting on the couch.

"Andy, June," said DI O'Dowd "we have carried out a PNC check on the registration number of the car found in the loch and the car is registered to Brian Berger, there were four deceased in the car and at this time we suspect that they are Brian, Sandra, and Susan along with Sheena Gough. Later today we are going to have to get formal identification of all the deceased before the post-mortem."

Andy said "please listen to this" as he played the recorded message from Brain Berger that was left for him. Both the DI and DS listened intently with their heads bowed.

"Listen, there are plenty of us that know all the deceased so we shall arrange the formal identification between us, there is no need for either of you to attend the mortuary," said DI O'Dowd.

"Thank you both for your kindness," said Andy.

They looked at June sitting on the edge of the couch with her arms folded across her stomach and bent over rocking back and forth staring at the floor.

As the officers were leaving June felt a hand of reassurance on her shoulder "take care June" said DS Anderson.

Andy closed the door quietly behind the officers so that he would not disturb the neighbours. Strangely, despite his grief, he felt for the two men that had just left his flat as they had to be the bearers of the news that they brought.

Andy wandered about aimlessly before going into his bedroom alone.

As he lay on the bed that he shared with Susan twenty-four hours earlier he could smell her perfume on her pillow and the bedsheet. The tears streamed down onto his pillow. Everything that they had dreamed of for their future had been wiped out in an instant by a monster of a father.

June lay on the couch on her own in disbelief that someone she thought she knew and loved could be so cruel to others and be part of such a group of people who used and abused children who needed love and care. Her tears were divided between Sheena and Susan, there were none for Brian or Sandra Berger that was for sure.

8 am

Andy sat at the table arms folded in front of himself leaning on the table, no tea or coffee, no toast with jam, he just sat staring out of the window. The Ford Granada with his minder was nowhere to be seen. There was no replacement. To Andy, it was if the whole enquiry had come to a sudden halt. The whole situation was surreal. All he could hear was the telephone ringing

"Andy?"

"Yes," he replied into the telephone.

"It's DS Anderson."

"Hi."

"Andy take as much time as you need mate, we shall extend your secondment."

"Thank you."

"Is June there?"

"Yes, I think so."

"What do you mean?"

"I have not seen her this morning."

"If she is there tell her the same please everything has been sorted."

"Yeah sure, thank you for calling Sergeant," he said hanging up the phone.

Andy went into the spare room having knocked on the door, getting no reply. He found June curled up on the bed awake.

"June I am going to see Susan."

"Can I come with you please?" she asked.

"Why would you want to do that?"

"I want to be there for you."

"Thank you" he replied.

As Andy parked at the mortuary, he switched off the engine of his car and sat silently.

"Are you sure about this mate?"

"Yes, June" replied Andy.

The mortuary attendant that Andy had got to know so well over the past couple of years, looked at Andy with a sadness in his eyes. He respectfully pulled back the white sheet that was covering Susan folding it neatly at her shoulders, before walking away leaving Andy and June alone in their moment of grief. Susan looked asleep and so peaceful. Andy placed his hand on the glass partition his tears running silently over his cheeks.

Although Sheena lay in the same mortuary June had no wish to see her.

As they were about the leave the car park, they saw a vehicle arrive with the Divisional Commander, Ralph McGrory driving.   He accompanied a man and woman into the mortuary. Waiting until they left, a short time later, Andy went back into the mortuary where he saw Chris, the attendant.

"Who were the couple that was just in here," he asked.

"Hang on I shall look for you Andy they took property away with them except an engagement ring."

"That belongs to Susan I bought her that I shall sign for it," he said receiving the ring from Chris and signing the property register.

"That couple were Colin Berger, brother of the deceased Brian Berger, and his wife Alison."

"Thank you."

"Andy they are going to make all the funeral arrangements for Brian, Sandra and Susan I don't know what is happening with the other deceased."

"Thanks" he replied before making his way back to his car and June.

Passing through Bankvale Andy noticed that the school was closed, he later learned that had been arranged by the head-teacher as a mark of respect to Susan. A mark of respect for a well-loved teacher.

Andy and June went back to his flat. The phone calls had been numerous and showed ten missed calls. Friends and colleagues had left messages of condolences. Then there was the tearful call from Alice asking Andy to contact her or Ricky as soon as possible.

Andy called his brother's house and got Alice who could hardly speak to him through floods of tears. Ricky then took over and offered his condolences and an invite for Andy to stay with them which Andy declined but was thankful for the offer.

Andy informed June that the Berger family were arranging the funerals for Brian, Sandra, and Susan and as far as he knew nothing had been arranged for Sheena. June informed Andy that her mother was elderly, but she had a brother somewhere and she would try and find him.

June left Andy alone in his flat as she returned home to her house and begin the quest of finding Sheena's brother. She decided to go to the home of Sheena's mother later that day. On her arrival, a police vehicle sat outside, and officers were leaving the house. She waited until they left the street before knocking on the door. A tall dark-haired man answered,

"Can I help you?" he said.

"I am June Brown a friend to Sheena."

"Ah I have heard of you please come in I am Simon Gough her brother."

"I am so sorry for your loss."

"So, what is your connection to Sheena."

"We were close friends" was June's reply.

"Nice that she had someone in her life," he said.

"Can I give you my phone number please."

"Certainly, and we shall contact you with arrangements."

"Thank you," said June as she left the house after a brief visit.

As the day went on the brandy in the bottle got less and less as Andy slowly got himself into a drunken state. He eventually fell asleep on the couch that he shared so many times with Susan.

Near to midnight there was banging on the door which wakened Andy and he slowly rose from the couch thinking Susan had forgotten her keys. Then reality struck him that it could not be Susan.

Looking through the spyhole on the door he saw June standing on the landing.

"Christ Andy look at the state of you," she said.

"Why are you here?"

"Have you not had the news on?"

"No."

"Andy they are treating it as an accident."

"June it was not an accident listen again to this again."

Andy played the message from Brian Berger again that he had left on the answering machine.

"Andy who knows about that message."

"Only you and I, the DI and DS at the moment."

"Andy where is the envelope given to you by Kerry."

"It is well hidden away."

"Good." She said as she sat down.

An open box lay on a small table. An engagement ring that had been worn by Susan sat neatly in the blue velvet box.

June poured black coffee into Andy to get him to sober up a bit. "I am going to stay here with you tonight to make sure you don't have any more to drink. Tomorrow we shall go over the contents of the envelope."

Andy said to June that there was something he had to do to bring closure for Susan and himself also.

Chapter Nine

Andy awoke with a stinking hangover from the amount of Brandy he had consumed, and he began the day by drinking lots of water to rehydrate himself while the percolator bubbled.

"Is that coffee I smell?" Asked June who had stayed overnight in the spare room.

"Yes, it is," said Andy.

"Okay," was her reply.

June sat at the table where Susan used to sit. There was a silence in the room as Andy and June gazed out of the large bay window. Andy said that as soon as the funerals were over, he would be leaving the flat even though he was there before Susan had moved in with him, but he felt he could no longer be in there without her. As he looked around little bits of Susan were everywhere, the way she sorted the cushions, where she had left her perfume bottle on a table before taking her mother home. June watched Andy closely as the tears rolled down his face. She placed her hand on top of his to comfort him.

Andy got dressed and made a telephone call finding out where Susan was resting at the undertakers.

Leaving June in the flat he drove into the city and introduced himself to the undertaker who showed him into a waiting room. Andy spoke with the undertaker who then led him to the chapel of rest where Susan lay. The undertaker left Andy with Susan. He walked around the open coffin and took Susan's left hand in his and placed their engagement ring on her finger for the second and last time. He leaned forward and kissed her forehead in one final goodbye kiss. This was the last time Andy would ever see Susan Berger as he closed the door behind him.

When Andy got back to the flat there was a familiar vehicle sitting outside on the road at his close.

He opened the door to the living room; June was sitting with DS Anderson and DI O'Dowd. June said to Andy that she had contacted them to let them hear the message on the answering machine again from Brian Berger.

"They have something to tell you, Andy," said June staring at the floor, tears streaming down her face.

"Andy this is being treated as a tragic accident caused by a fault in the brakes on Brian's car," said DS Anderson

"Are you telling me that even with that message it was an accident?" asked Andy as his eyes narrowed looking at them both in disbelief

"Yes Andy," replied DI O'Dowd then pausing before imparting the rest of the information. "There shall be no criminal enquiry, it is a traffic enquiry into a fatal accident" he continued while looking at Andy and June. He appeared uncomfortable, almost nervous, delivering what seemed to be a rehearsed speech that he had been told what to say to them. Andy stood silent for a moment or two taking in what had been said to him. DI O'Dowd, standing there with all his years' service, was not liking this role he had been given. Andy had a gut feeling he was not there by choice.

"Three murders and a suicide become an accident?" asked Andy in a calm voice.

"Take time to yourself and you can come back to work after the funeral," said DI O'Dowd avoiding the question

"Thank you," replied Andy.

"June that goes for you also I have spoken to your Sergeant."

"Thank you" replied June.

DI O'Dowd turned to Andy and June as he was leaving with DS Anderson, he looked at both, for a split second Andy felt some sympathy for him and Liam Anderson, "Listen, guys, we know you are hurting and angry, but this is out of my hands," he said as he closed the door stepping out onto the stairhead landing watched by Andy.

Andy went into the bedroom and returned with the envelope, the one given to him by Kerry.

He handed the envelope to June who opened it carefully and took out the contents, a diary with some instant photographs clearly showing the faces of the participants engaged in sexual behaviour. The contents of the diary carefully written detailed all the players of the games. Their sexual preferences and age groups of the girls or boys they desired. Each of the parties, giving the venue and times were also detailed.

Months and months of entries had been noted and it took Andy and June some considerable time to go over every detail. Closing the diary, shocked by what they read and of those involved. June slipped the diary and photographs back into the envelope and Andy took it back to its place of concealment.

"What next Andy?"

"I was just about to ask you the same thing."

"So, neither of us know then," said Andy.

"See at the end of the day Kerry has entrusted us to look after this diary, she trusted us to bring these people down, but we cannot do this alone," he said.

"You know if the bosses knew or anyone knew we had this we would be finished Andy once and for all."

"Yes, and you have too much service to lose that June, is there anyone we can trust with all this."

"I don't know to be honest."

"Okay, I shall keep it for now and see how things go."

"Fine," said June.

"I better go home to my place and try and get back to normal if there is such a thing after all this, what are you going to do?" June asked.

"I shall go see Mum at Ricky and Alice's."

"Okay, big man I shall be in touch," she said as she left the flat.

When Andy had closed the door, he stood leaning his back against it with his hands behind him and his eyes closed, "Listen, guys, we know you are hurting and angry, but this is out of my hands," those were the parting words by DI O'Dowd, so, if the deaths were out of his hands, whose hands were they in? who decided to call this an accident? Who examined the vehicle and deemed that it was brake failure? Why are they ignoring the message on my answering machine? he thought to himself before going into his bedroom and falling asleep.

The drive from his flat to the east end the following morning was one that he was not looking forward too at all as he had to break the news of Susan's' death to his mother who was already fragile added to the fact that he did not know what reception he was going to get from his brother considering the recent history between them. He pressed the intercom at the sprawling gates to the Blackmore villa and watched as the gates opened.

"Come in Andy," said Alice, as she pulled him close and hugged him tightly.

"I am so, so sorry Andy I truly am," she said.

"Thank you" he whispered to her.

"Andy," said Ricky as he held out both arms to greet his brother, Andy and Ricky held each other. This was not what he was expecting.

"This is a so sad Andy I am gutted for you, I know we have our differences, but this is different."

"Thank you, both of you, where is Mum?" he asked.

"She is in the living room," replied Ricky.

"Andy walked in and saw his mum sitting alone."

He kneeled in front of her and she looked into his eyes and even though she was fading into her own small world day by day she could see the sadness in his eyes.

"Hello, son have you brought that nice girl with you?"

"No mum" he paused.

"Why the tears Andrew?" she asked running the back of her frail hand down his cheek.

"Mum, Susan has been killed she is no longer with us."

"Oh, dear such a lovely girl," was her gentle response.

She reached out as Andy placed his head on her lap and felt his mother's hand stroking the side of his face as she did so many years ago when he was a child and needed comforting. They remained like that for several minutes. "Mum I will be back soon, I promise, "he said. Slowly, Andy straightened himself up and wiped his face before he walked back through to see Ricky and Alice.

"I have something to tell you both and being quite honest Ricky, I don't care what you say, or to whom, about this, Brian Berger, murdered his wife, daughter and Sheena Gough, and he committed suicide."

Ricky and Alice sat stunned at what Andy had said.

"How do you know; do you have proof?" asked Ricky.

"On the news, they said it was a tragic accident due to a brake failure," said Alice.

"Sorry for this Andy but is this is part of your conspiracy theory again to keep things quiet."

"Ricky," said Alice annoyed at her husband.

Andy looked at Ricky and Alice and told them of the telephone call from Brian Berger just before he drove into the Loch.

"I take it your colleagues have heard the message."

"Yes, and they have said it is out of their hands it was an accident."

"Leave it, Andy, let Susan rest in peace," said Ricky.

"Do you know, of all the times and places he could have murdered them, he chose a night I was working, and in the area, I was working, he would know we would attend the locus, just to rub salt into the wound of taking my Susan's life, how evil is that?"

Ricky and Alice sat quietly and said nothing to Andy's last comment. Alice placed three black coffees on the worktop in the kitchen. Andy stared into his watching it spin around in the cup as he stirred in the sugar. Andy explained that he would not rest until each and everyone involved in this scandal was behind bars and if he could not do it then he would have to make alternative plans.

The alternative plans comment shook Ricky, he suggested to Andy that he had to think that his probation had not long finished and that he was not a seasoned detective with years of experience and to take on such an establishment with all its internal friendships would be like taking on Goliath. He added that he thought this enquiry could or would cost Andy his job one way or another. Andy sat quietly taking his brothers words onboard and thinking about who held the aces in this pack. He felt he held all the aces then made a decision that would make or break the whole case, but he had to speak to Kerry one more time. Before he left the villa they exchanged thoughts about their mother, and it was decided that they would deal with everything regarding her future very soon. Andy then drove back to his flat and abandoned his car before walking to the pub to look for Kerry only to be told that she had finished weeks ago and that as far as anyone knew she was in Europe hitch-hiking before going to University. To lose Kerry now was a major blow to him and the enquiry.

As he opened the door to his flat there was just a wall of silence, that bubbly welcome home had gone, that welcome kiss had gone, that hug had gone, Brian Berger had robbed him of everything he loved. As he sat there alone thinking he decided.......

"Can I speak to Mr David Diamond please?" asked Andy making the telephone that was to change everything in the weeks to come

"Who is calling?" asked a lady

"Just tell him it is a friend."

"I am sorry sir I need a name before he will take your call."

"Tell him I have something explosive and exclusive for him unseen by anyone, and I will take it elsewhere if I have to," said Andy forcefully

"David here" came the urgent voice on the phone.

"Mr Diamond I need to speak to you."

"Who is this please?"

"I have information that could lead to the downfall of Senior figures in public life, are you interested?"

"Depends, what you have and who you are."

"Okay, I know you by sight for obvious reasons so, go to the Golden Thistle tonight, be there for nine pm I shall give you a small sample of what I have to offer you then it's your call as to whether you want to take this on. What shall be said to you is "Brian sent me" do you understand?"

"I shall have to think about this" replied Diamond wondering if he was being set up by a hoaxer.

"Well don't think too long I am gone at nine-fifteen pm."

Andy stuffed the envelope down the back of his jeans and made his way back into the city by train. He pushed open the door to the Golden Thistle, bought a pint of heavy, he scanned the pub but there was no sign of Diamond anywhere. He sat at a table facing the door waiting to see if Diamond would come in.

At nine-fifteen pm Andy stood up to leave the pub and made his way towards the door as it opened inwards and in walked televisions most experienced investigative reporter, David Diamond the man who had exposed more wrongdoing on television than any other investigative reporter. "Excuse me" as he brushed past Andy heading for the bar looking at his watch and around the bar anxiously knowing he had possibly missed his appointment.

Andy went back to the bar and purchased a Brandy before sitting down again. He looked around again trying to ascertain if there were any police in the bar watching him or if Diamond had been followed maybe by some of his team. He had no idea how this worked at all.

Diamond was constantly looking at his watch as it drifted towards nine-thirty. He went into the Gents toilet followed by Andy. Diamond was standing at the urinal as Andy pushed open a cubicle door to ensure it was empty then stood next to Diamond.

"Brian sent me." sending the message to Diamond.

"I thought you would be well gone," he replied.

"No, I have been watching you, everything and everyone around you."

"Who are you?" asked Diamond.

"Someone who needs you, let's go back inside we need to talk."

"What about?"

"I am about to show you," replied Andy.

"Whisky for me please," David asked the barman "and what about you?" he asked Andy as they stood at the bar.

"Brandy please."

As they lifted their drinks Andy immediately sat with his back to the wall with a clear view of the door watching for anyone that resembled someone watching him.

"Well?" asked Diamond.

Andy reached into the back of his jeans and removed the envelope. He produced an instant photograph which showed the faces of men engaged in sexual activity with a young girl which he handed to Diamond.

"Where did you get this?" asked Diamond.

"Sorry I can't say."

"Who are you?"

"Sorry I can't say."

"What can you say?"

"Get justice for her and others."

"Listen do you know who these guys are?"

"Yes."

"These are powerful people in this photograph?" said Diamond stunned by the image he was holding.

"I have a load of photographs with many more faces."

"Anything else?"

"Yes, diary, places, dates, names, everything you need."

"How much do you want?"

"Now that is something I have never thought about."

"Everyone thinks of money name your price?" Said Diamond with a tone Andy hated.

Andy sat and thought for a few moments looking at the small table in front of him and tapping it with his finger deep in thought. "I know," he said

"Okay, go for it" replied Diamond

"You shall sponsor the Susan Berger, Student of the Year Trophy at Bankvale High School, I shall call you tomorrow at three pm I shall use the name Jethro and you shall accept the call I await your decision as to the financial arrangements."

Andy got up and walked out of the pub taking the photograph with him. David Diamond watched him as he left. Was this guy a joker or was he for real? was his thought. Usually, people wanted a lot of money for what he allegedly had but this guy just wanted a trophy for a school, all seemed a bit strange to him, he just had to wait and see if this guy he knew as Jethro followed through on his call.

At three o'clock the following day, on time, Andy made his call. He was immediately put through to David Diamond when he identified himself as "Jethro" Diamond agreed to the "fee" then told Andy that he knew who Susan Berger was and the reason for the request for a trophy in her name. Andy knew that he would follow up the Susan Berger name and that it would not take him long to put one and one together. Arrangements were made for a further meeting in a very isolated area that Andy choose to ensure that neither were followed. His location was on a hillside overlooking the loch where Susan had died. "eleven am tomorrow, be there I shall reveal everything I have to you," said Andy.

Andy was there early; he had a clear view of the road surrounding the meeting point. There was no way that Diamond could be followed without him knowing as the single-track road ran from one side of the hillside to the other with a few passing places strategically placed along the way.

Having parked his car, he had made his way up the hillside on foot, high enough to keep watch. His target was arriving and parked behind Andy's car. He watched as Diamond made his way up the hillside.

"You don't make this easy, do you?" asked Diamond.

"No."

"Well, what do you have for me after all this?"

About an hour later after having examined everything Diamond turned to Andy who he only knew as 'Jethro' and admitted what he had seen was explosive, to say the least. Diamond was told that he could take notes from the diary and list everyone that he knew in the photographs as the diary was not going with him.

I look forward to hearing from you "Jethro" handing back the diary and photographs. "David you will never hear from me again," said Andy as he walked away down the hillside and got into his car before driving off.

Arriving back in his flat he hoped that David Diamond was the man to get justice for Susan, not only her but Kerry and all the others. He prayed that Kerry would forgive him for sharing the information she entrusted him with for safekeeping.

Andy pressed the play button on his answering machine. "Andy this is DS Anderson, just to let you know that Susan's funeral will be at two-thirty on Wednesday, it will be a triple funeral with her mother and father at the city crematorium in the east end, I know that you knew Sheena also, hers shall be at the same place at three-thirty. Before that, there is a service at East End Old Parish Church at one pm."

Andy phoned June to make sure she was aware of the arrangements for the funeral which she was, and they agreed that they would travel together for both services. They also agreed to go to the church service together.

As Andy sat in his flat his telephone rang.

"Hello," said Andy.

"Andy I am sorry to bother you this is Colin Berger."

"How can I help you, sir?"

"My wife and I found your phone number in Brian and Sandra's phone book."

"Oh Okay."

"We have been told by their neighbours you were Susan's boyfriend."

"We were engaged," said Andy.

"Oh, Andy I am so sorry, we did not know that this makes this even more sensitive then."

"What does?"

"Okay, I am doing a eulogy for Brian and Sandra would you do one for Susan."

"Thank you, it would be an honour."

"Wonderful I am doing mine at the church would you do yours at the crematorium."

"Yes sir"

"Thank you, Andy, see you there on Wednesday at the church."

Andy sat down on their couch and started to prepare a eulogy for Susan. Two hours later it would be complete. Andy said nothing to anyone that he had been asked to deliver the eulogy to the congregation, not even June.

On the day of the funerals, Andy picked up June at noon in his car which was gleaming from a fresh wash and polish.

"Geez Andy all shiny today," she said trying to lift their spirits as the dark rain clouds gathered above them.

"Yeah Susan said this was a mobile skip so did this for today" as he drove off heading for his home territory.

They arrived at the Old Parish Church at twelve forty-five pm, The pavements on both sides of the road was mobbed with mourners from all walks of life including many of Susan's colleagues who had arrived by bus from Bankvale. Parking spaces were at a premium, but Andy being an east end boy was prepared for this and had arranged to park his car in an old friends driveway a few minutes' walking distance from the church. As Andy and June approached the entrance they saw serving and retired police officers milling around. Some were in uniform some not. Andy's' presence there did not go unnoticed by many current and retired senior officers. Thankfully, the old red sandstone building would be big enough to accommodate everyone.

Three hearses arrived at the entrance to the church at twelve-fifty pm. "Mr Blackmore, Miss Brown, please follow me," said a man who appeared to be part of the undertakers' entourage who had been handing out order of ceremony cards as the congregation entered the church. Andy looked at June and shrugged his shoulder unaware of why they were been led down the aisle. "Here sir," said the man showing Andy and June their seats on the front pew beside Susan's Aunt and Uncle who smiled at them as they sat down. The coffins remained in the vehicles during the service. Colin Berger gave a beautiful eulogy to his brother and sister-in-law possibly unaware of the background to the days' events. As the mourners left the church June said that she thought it was strange that Colin said virtually nothing about Susan. Andy informed her that was to come at the crematorium it was a matter of time at each venue. She accepted his story without question.

On arrival at the crematorium, Andy watched as Susan and her parents arrived together. He saw Ricky and Alice there and acknowledged them with a nod of the head. June was by his side.

As the coffins were taken from the cars Andy moved forward and excused one of the coffin bearers.

"This is the last chance I shall get to be with my fiancée may I carry her down the aisle?" he asked. The pallbearer stood aside.

As each of the coffins was laid side by side DI O'Dowd, DS Anderson and many of Andy's colleagues had watched on as he carried Susan's body into the West Chapel. Many were in silent tears.

Following the hymn "Abide with me" Reverend MacDonald announced that there was to be a eulogy for Susan to be read by her fiancée Andrew Blackmore.

A television crew with a discrete camera were filming for the news to be broadcast later that night. This was Andy's chance to right all the wrongs in public and make the funeral news headlines for all the wrong reasons. He owed that to Kerry, but he owed more to Susan.

Andy rose from his seat and made his way to the pulpit. He scanned the mourners recognising face after face from the photographs. His Detective Inspector and Detective Sergeant sat with bated breath wondering what the 'Iceberg', the loose cannon, was about to say in public. June and Alice watched with pride as he had been asked to deliver this moment to all by Colin Berger. Ricky stared at the pulpit not knowing what to expect from his brother.

Andy's eulogy began in silence. He looked at all seated before him. He looked at the coffins to his right-hand side. He gave a long lingering look at Susan's coffin with its red roses on top that he had purchased especially for the service. His card on the flowers read simply "Freebird". Freebird was a song that they loved listening to late at night. There was a wreath from her school propped against the coffin with the school crest on it and the words "Forever Young" printed on the card. The power of Andy's silence could be felt across the rows of pews. "Ladies and Gentlemen" he began slowly in a low voice. "My name is Andy Blackmore and I have been asked to deliver this eulogy, by Colin and Alison Berger for Susan" he reached into his inside jacket pocket, removing the folded pages containing his eulogy then laying it on the lectern. Andy knew the eulogy off by heart as he briefly gazed at the introduction.

"It is easy to stand here at a time like this and wax lyrically about someone who is no longer here and about how great he or she was in life. It is what people want to hear. It is not always true, so putting this together last night sitting alone in my flat, our flat, I wondered what Susan would have wanted me to say and write it in her words, it is not something that we discussed as we thought we had many years ahead of us until that cruel and fateful night tore us apart. I think Susan would have wanted something simple, like, tell them we were at school together and you fancied me, which raised some laughter in the chapel, or tell them that Susan fell head over heels for a young police officer when she first set eyes on him after years apart at Bankvale High School when he came to make enquiries about a case he was involved in. You can tell them how we got engaged at Christmas and spent loads of nights curled up on the beat-up old couch that was so comfortable for us to snuggle up together and make plans for the future, I think that is what Susan would have wanted me to say"

As he looked around, he could hear little bits of laughter from her friends seated nearby among the sobbing from others.

"What I want to say personally is that Susan Berger was, and still is the love of my life. I said to her when I gave her the keys to my flat, "Mi casa es su casa". It still is, as much of her items are still there. I am sure Susan's friends and colleagues, many of whom are here today, shall always treasure her memory in the years to come for her dedication to teaching and helping others less fortunate than herself. She was never a boastful person in any way, shape, or form, but from what I have been told she had a brilliant future ahead of her."

Andy looked around the chapel again, both detectives, O'Dowd and Anderson were watching him intently. Those that did not know him before the ceremony, now knew who was speaking to them from the pulpit having introduced himself at the beginning of the eulogy.

"Susan and I were in our local pub recently, a young lady approached our table and referred to her as Miss Berger. Susan immediately recognised her. That young lady said to Susan "You were my inspiration at school, so much so I am now going to university to study to be a teacher like you" he paused, "Susan was so proud of that young lady who was brought up in a children's home and had come good despite everything she had faced in her short life and against all the odds. Her name was Kerry and some of you here may know of her, so Kerry if you are out there, as Susan said to you that night don't be like me, be you" and what I can say is, that Kerry is exactly how Susan wanted her to be. "Susan," he said looking at her coffin, "Kerry would now be your hero if you know what I mean, I am sure that you do my love." Andy stood in silence looking around him. "That was the measure of Susan always thinking of others."

"Thank you for your attention ladies and gentlemen," said Andy leaving the pulpit.

He stood in front of the coffin and bowed his head in honour of Susan and placed his hand on it, a final goodbye.

He never even glanced at the coffins of Brian and Sandra and that did not go unnoticed by some of the congregation. The final paragraph Andy delivered, sent out a message to many and they all knew that he knew the truth about the crimes and offences they had been involved in.

Andy sat back down beside June, her hand clasped his, and he felt a soft squeeze of support. Joe and Georgie were seated behind him and he felt a hand tap his shoulder, a hand of support from Joe.

As the minister brought the service to a close with "The Lord is my Shepherd" the curtains closed on the coffins. Mourners slowly made their way from the small chapel which awaited the arrival of the remains of Sheena Gough.

June, Joe, Georgie, and Andy stood outside the chapel talking. DI O'Dowd and DS Anderson approached and shook Andy by the hand and congratulated him on his eulogy.

"You got your message out there Andy loud and clear well done," said DS Anderson.

"What does that mean Sergeant?" asked Joe.

"I think he means about Susan being a wonderful human being Joe," said June.

"Exactly" replied DS Anderson.

Andy was very aware that some people were looking in his direction and talking, there was a lot of worried faces standing on that car park and the strain was showing on others as they made their way to their cars.

"Andy may we have a word please," said Colin Berger accompanied by his wife.

"That was beautiful, and we would like to thank you."

"Susan was beautiful and no matter what I said here today could match that are you coming to the reception?" asked Colin

"Yes, we shall but we have another friend to see off first. I say we as it is my turn to support June."

"Oh, who is that?"

"Sheena Gough, who was also in the car."

"Oh, dear dear, please join us when you can," said Alison.

Ricky and Alice came over and both gave Andy a hug of support as they knew he was hurting deep inside. They declined an invite to the reception as they had to go back home for their children.

They watched as friends and colleagues departed the scene, some going back to work, some heading for the local hotel where the reception was being held. Andy stood solid by June's side as the hearse carrying the remains of Sheena could be seen down the long winding driveway then stopping for a few moments until their allotted arrival time. Directly behind the hearse was a large black car carrying her mother, her brother, and other close members of the family.

As the hearse drew to a halt outside the chapel the family made their way inside. Simon Gough acknowledged the presence of June with a bow of his head as he helped his mother. The service was a simple affair. Simon Gough delivered the eulogy to his sister in a touching manner. Andy could feel that June was very tense throughout the proceedings and until the service finished.

June introduced Andy to Simon as a colleague of hers and they shook hands.

"Andy, I believe your fiancée was in the car also."

"Yes, sir."

"Such a shame, do you know what, I can't help wondering why they were all together."

"I know Sandra was a friend of Sheena's," said Andy

"Yes, more than a friend from what I have heard. Something does not ring true with this Andy."

"Like what, sir?"

"I just don't know yet."

"Sir can you excuse us we have somewhere to go."

"June I shall be in touch I would like to speak to you," said Simon Gough

"Certainly, you have my phone number," was her response.

. As they walked away Andy said to June that he thought Simon was onto something and not likely to rest any time soon. Andy asked June if she would prefer to go to the reception for Sheena, but she was aware that the family were having a small private gathering at her mothers' house for family only.

A very short time later, Andy and June stood at the entrance to the reception area in the nearby hotel. Andy took a long deep breath before entering as he expected to see some faces that he recognised. June felt the same pressure as they walked in together. Andy was not sure if it was his imagination, but the atmosphere seemed to change a little with their presence. People huddled together, the small talk went around the room, glances were thrown in their direction. Andy suggested to June they act as normal as possible as if they know nothing at all.

"Andy, June please join us," said Colin "Would you like a drink?"

"We shall join you certainly, but I shall pass on the alcohol," said Andy.

They sat down together at the table reserved for the Berger family. Andy and June both knew they were in the company of some well-known people who were friends of Brian and Sandra and instantly recognisable from the photographs. They listened to the stories and times they shared with Brian and Sandra through their various careers and how they had helped each out along the way making their lives successful and comfortable for the age they were now at in retirement.

Andy decided to throw a hand grenade into the chatter to see the response he would get.

"Tell me I seem to know a few of you for some reason," he said. June could not believe what she was hearing for a moment

"Oh, how is that then," said one of the men seated at the table.

"It's just, em, I know Brian and Sandra used to go to Games Nights with friends and I have seen some of the photographs from their nights out some of you look familiar"

There was a sudden silence around the table. June sat motionlessly and could not believe Andy had brought this up at this time. Colin Berger broke the silence saying he had heard Brian and Sandra were going to Games Nights but from his recollections, he was not the sporting type although he did like playing cards.

"Yes, he loved a game of whist," said one man "then again so did Sandra they were good at it."

Everything seemed to become very awkward at the table as Andy excused himself to go to the Gents toilet. Standing at the urinal he became aware of a presence behind him. He took his time before finishing off and turning around.

"Gentlemen, please remember where you are and that this is a funeral reception," he said looking at the three men in their fifties.

"Mr Blackmore," said the larger of the men, standing well over six feet tall of heavy build and receding hairline, but every inch of him indicated that he was retired police officer. "Listen to me"

"You have me at a disadvantage, you know me, I don't know you," said Andy interrupting.

"Well let me introduce myself as retired Superintendent James Oliver."

"Pleased to meet you," replied Andy flippantly.

"I doubt it" replied Oliver.

"No seriously, I like to put names to faces," he said looking at Oliver before pausing.

"Now if you shall excuse me, I have a funeral reception to return to gentlemen," he said drying his hands.

As Andy went to make his way out of the door the retired Superintendent raised his hand putting it on Andy's chest.

"Please don't do that sir" Andy requested looking him in the eyes.

"Why?"

"Because I am asking and normally, I only do that once," he said calmly.

"Listen here young man, you have caused a lot of people a lot of grief and worry, it stops now" he demanded in a threatening tone of voice.

"I have asked you once sir, I shall not ask again take your hand away from me sir."

"Make me" replied Oliver staring at Andy.

Before the retired Superintendent could move his hand, Andy had knocked it away and had a tight grip on James Oliver's testicles. A favourite target of Andy's.

"Now guys unless Mr Oliver here likes crushed nuts, I suggest you both go into a cubicle and lock the doors, now."

Andy gave a slight squeeze increasing the pressure.

"Do what he says," said Oliver in a strained voice.

The snib on the doors could be heard going into the locking position as Oliver's face reddened.

"Now you listen to me Mr Oliver, prison is not a good place for an ex-cop from what I hear so you are going to be my bitch in the absence of Mr Brian Berger do you understand?"

"I hear you."

"I know you do but you better be listening" as Andy released his grip and left the toilet.

"Everything Okay Andy?" enquired June as Andy sat down beside her

"Just Dandy" he replied as June saw the three men leave the Gents together and exiting the reception.

Andy excused himself from the Berger table as did June. They both shook hands with Colin and Alison. Andy gave Colin his phone number should he need anything in the coming weeks.

"I shall be in touch," said Colin.

As Andy and June left the reception he turned and looked at James Oliver who was holding court with many others. His departure was noted by all.

Andy dropped off June at her place then he made his way back to his flat where he put on the television. There was some coverage of the funeral was on the news along with a few lines from his eulogy for Susan. Andy took off his suit which he hung up in the wardrobe along with his black tie. His shirt went straight into the washing machine. Andy was back in casual gear.

He made his way down to the pub where he was greeted by local friends some of whom knew Susan and were at the funeral. They were still in their suits from earlier on and accompanied by their wives and girlfriends.

As Andy stood at the bar with his back to everyone a man stood beside him as the barmaid handed Andy his drinks. The man produced a ten-pound note and said, "I shall pay for these and I shall have a pint of lager."

"Hello Jethro or should I say, Mr Blackmore," said David Diamond. Andy looked around the pub and found a table in the corner where they both walked to in silence and sat down together.

"Now what can I do for you David?"

"Oh, Andy it is what I can do for you, to be honest, you are going to get that trophy in memory of Susan, and it shall be competed for this year and annually for the student of the year"

"Thank You"

"Now to business," said David……..

Chapter Ten

A week after Susan's funeral, Andy was back at his desk. He had given much thought to throw the towel in and resign from the force, he had been down this road before and was stopped by June and Sergeant Black who had much faith in him. Sitting alone in his flat, on their beloved old couch, Andy considered his options on his future, do I go and return to the building sites, leaving behind many unanswered questions that nobody will ever give me answer to, or, do I stay seek answers to everything and fight this rotten system from within. He decided to stay and fight.

"Andy can you come into my office please," asked DS Anderson.

"Sure" getting up from his desk and following the Sergeant into his office

They both sat down, and the door opened. In walked DI O'Dowd. He threw a file onto the desk.

"Well Andy boy, life about here without you is going to be dull that is for sure. This is your final assessment from us. We see you have not sat your promotion exams yet any reason why?"

"Well just with everything that has happened it was the last thing on my mind,"

"That is understandable, shall you be doing them next time around?"

"I don't know, to be honest, I just take everything one day at a time now."

"We hope that you do as we would like to have you back here as soon as possible."

"Thank you."

"Now Andy," said the DI, I have to accompany you to the Divisional Commanders office."

"Do you know why sir?"

"I know as much as you."

"Okay, let's do it," said Andy

Andy and his DI sat outside the Divisional Commanders office with his assistant watching over them. The telephone rang which she answered, "Yes Sir" she said replacing the receiver.

"Gentlemen you may go in now,"

Andy followed his DI into the office. "take a seat please" said McGrory.

McGrory sat looking at both officers before breaking his silence. "I have a letter here from the Procurators Fiscal office, I shall not go into the full letter but basically what it says is that the Crown Office having considered all the evidence presented at this time about the abuse of children and the deaths of some individuals allegedly connected to the enquiry, they believe that they shall not be taking any proceedings against any individual or individuals named in the reports as it is not in the public interest or the interests of the children, unless, further evidence is found." Andy and his DI sat silently. Gentlemen, I am telling you this because I believe tonight there is or was going to be a television programme broadcast by David Diamond making serious allegations against several people. Lawyers are in touch with the television programme-makers, and, as we speak trying to get the programme taken off the air. Do either of you wish to comment especially you Andy as you always have something to say?"

"What is the date of the letter sir?"

"It is dated for yesterday, why did you ask that?"

"No reason. Thank you, sir."

"If there's nothing else gents, I am a busy man," dismissing them unceremoniously from his office.

"Well sir there is, to be honest," said Andy causing DI O'Dowd to glance in his direction.

"Make it quick Blackmore as I said I am a busy man," said an impatient McGrory, looking down at his desk shuffling papers.

"Okay, whose decision was it to take the enquiry into Susan's death out of the hands of the CID? Whose decision was it to declare that it was an accident? Who was the vehicle examiner who declared that it was a brake failure that caused the so-called accident and where is the vehicle now? Why was the message on my answering machine ignored by senior CID officers who heard the contents of that message?" asked Andy rattling out the questions one after the other.

McGrory stopped what he was doing and looked up, "Mr Blackmore the enquiry is over, as to who made the decisions about the direction the enquiry is nothing to do with you. Following the vehicle examination, by experienced vehicle examiners, that was photographed and removed from the garage by an authorised contractor and it has since been scrapped and crushed, now does that answer your questions"

"And the message on my telephone?" asked Andy.

"I know nothing about that, what call and from whom?" asked McGrory.

"No, you are right sir, this enquiry is over" replied Andy being watched closely by Detective Inspector O'Dowd.

Both left the office, silently. Andy went straight into the Detective Constables room and cleared out his desk, ready to go back to his shift and back into uniform. He filed away the unsolved vandalisms he had been nursing for months. Bobby, Danny, and Gordon knew there was something wrong, very wrong by Andy's silence and demeanour. Nobody said anything as Bobby went to see the DI.

A short time later, Bobby returned to the office breaking the news to the others. "I am so sorry mate," he said.

"Maybe, maybe I just expected someone to believe them and make a go of it, and to think, if Brian Berger knew it was all going to turn out like this, then Susan would still have been here. Time for a new start for me I think."

"What does that mean?" asked Danny.

"I planned annual leave for the next couple of weeks when I finished here."

"Is that your six months over already Andy?" asked big Gordon

"Yes, it is, and I want to thank you all even though we had our ups and downs from time to time."

"You have been a breath of fresh air in here," said Bobby

"I wonder who is next then?"

"I hear it is some young friend of the Divisional Commander," said Andy.

"Yeah Blackmore wind up to finish with," said Danny laughing.

Andy packed his bag and shook hands with the team.

"See before you go" said Yardley, "Remember the day I drove you through the village and you spoke to Hughie about break-ins and poaching, well I have checked all the crime reports and there has not been one house or shop done since you got here and when you made him your deputy" he said laughing.

"Never heard any of you complain when we got salmon for breakfast" was his parting shot as he left the office. "Seeya guys"

He stopped off to see Detective Sergeant Anderson

"Seeya, Sergeant," seeing DI O'Dowd sitting in the room.

"Yeah, good luck Andy" he replied.

"DI O'Dowd thank you, sir, for everything."

"You are welcome, lad, good luck with the rest of your enquiries Andy. Oh, by the way, that was clever asking for the date of the letter."

Andy smiled, slung his bag over his shoulder and walked down the corridor to the Divisional Headquarters exit door. He never looked back. I lost the battle he thought but I have not lost the war, bring it on. What Andy had seemed to miss was the wording of Detective Inspector O'Dowd's farewell greeting.

"There he goes," said retired Superintendent Oliver watching as Andy's car left the car park, "no mistakes this time and if he goes into a garage stay away from him" As the men watched Andy, the news came on the radio, the breaking news was the announcement from the Crown Office. The men looked at each other and smiled "Benny came through good then" said Oliver, "now this changes things lets go for a stand-down in the meantime"

Chapter Eleven

Andy went into his flat and took stock of what he had and where he was going in life. Without Susan, it was not far or fast. He had lost someone so close to him that it felt there was a large piece of him missing and could not be replaced. He knew he had to start clearing out her possessions and that was going to hurt. He also knew that Susan would not want him to be wallowing in sorrow for the rest of his life as he sat on their couch thinking about her. The doorbell rang.

"Hi, mate can you sign for this please?" asked the delivery driver handing Andy a large box.

"Sure, there you go, I was not expecting anything, to be honest."

"All the better then" he shouted running down the stairs to do his next delivery.

Andy carefully opened the box, on the red label it warned "open with care". He lifted out a gleaming silver trophy which was on a mahogany plinth with enough space on the silver ring around it to cover the winners' names for many years to come. The inscription on the front of the trophy on a plain background read, "The Susan Berger Trophy" and below that "Best Overall Student." Andy looked inside and around the box and found a small card. Written thereon was "As Promised" and signed "DD" Andy wrapped up the trophy and placed it carefully back into the packaging and large cardboard box. He was filled with pride that Susan would not be forgotten for a very long time to come. With the trophy safely in his possession, he decided that it was time to start going through Susan's possessions. Wiping away the tears as he went into the bedroom with a large bag, he opened the wardrobe to reveal Susan's clothes she had brought to the flat when she moved in. Carefully he took them off the hangers and folded them neatly before placing them into the bag. When he had finished, he pulled the zip closed. Everything had gone from there.

On the dressing table, her jewellery box lay unopened, that was somewhere he had never even considered opening when they were together, there was no need for him ever to go in there. He lifted the lid and there lay her watch, bracelets, rings, and other items she had collected over the years along with the diamond bracelet he had bought her for Christmas. What struck Andy was the scented smell as he opened the box as if Susan was in the room with him. He could feel her on his shoulder watching him. Maybe she was, causing him to look around, but she was nowhere to be seen, only her presence was there. This was a bridge too far for Andy and he closed the box. This was for another day he thought.

"June, I need a favour please," he said calling June on the telephone.

"Sure, name it" she replied.

"I need you to take a bag of Susan's clothing away from here as far as possible and hand it in to a charity shop for me. I am asking you because I don't want to know where you take it if that makes sense."

"Sure, anything for you big man I shall collect it tonight and deal with it in the morning."

"Thank you see you soon as he hung up the phone."

His next decision was to start looking around for a flat away from where he was. He had rented his flat for a couple of years while waiting to see if he was successful in his probationary period which had passed by now.

"Hiya come in," he said answering the door to his flat

"Hiya big guy, how are you?" said June kissing him on his cheek.

"I have my moments, to be honest"

"So, do I," said June.

"Today was a ball buster, to be honest, clearing out Susan's clothing. I went into her jewellery box but had to close that as I just couldn't cope with it, now, here is a thing with her mother and father gone what happens to the contents of that box who is entitled to that stuff?"

"Geez, Andy I don't know I suppose her Uncle and Aunt as next of kin."

"Okay, I shall call Colin and offer it to him."

"Have you got the bag for me mate."

"Yes," he replied.

"Tell you what when I clear out Sheena's stuff you can return the favour."

"Done deal" he replied.

"I never knew you guys lived together."

"We didn't, just, we had stuff here and there together."

"Take care of yourself."

"Yeah, you too big man" as she lifted the bag of Susan's belongings leaving the flat.

As the door got rattled within seconds Andy answered it immediately.

"Do you know something you big gorilla? I love you to bits as a mate," said June.

"You are mad as a tu'penny watch June" as he cupped her cheeks kissing her full on the lips.

"Oh my god, I have waited for that for so long."

"Beat it you nutter," he said as he shut the door. Andy went to the window overlooking the street and he watched June putting Susan's belongings onto the rear seat of her car. When she was getting into her car she looked up towards Andy and waved to him.

Andy watched as June drove out of the street and as she disappeared out of sight his telephone rang.

"Hello," Andy said answering the telephone.

"Andy this is Colin Berger I need to speak to you." sounding anxious.

"That is strange I need to speak to you also."

"Andy can you meet me at Brian's house."

"Sure when?"

"Tonight, and bring that woman officer with you"

"Who June?

"Yes, that is her name there is something you must both see."

"She has just left here I shall see what I can do."

Andy immediately telephoned June's house leaving a message for her.

"June when you get in, I am on my way to your house stay in until I get there."

Andy left the house immediately and made his way to June's house.

"Geezuz Andy I am just in two minutes in front of you what's up?" June said opening the door.

"I got a call from Colin Berger; he wants you and me at Brian's house tonight."

154

"No, Andy no, enough is enough, this is all over it is finished, finito, nada mas, mate."

"Really?" he said

"How many languages do you need me to use for you to understand it's over."

"Okay, I understand Italian and Spanish for finished and no more" he paused.

"If you can say it in double Dutch then I shall walk away," he said as he smiled at her.

"Andy, bloody, Blackmore you are impossible," she huffed.

"Okay, the last chapter in this book lets go," she said grabbing her house keys.

"Thank you, do you know I could not have a better mate in this job."

"This is not work, Andy this is private and personal now."

"Okay, I could not have a better private and personal mate right now," he said softly looking at June.

"Stop it, stop looking at me that way, let's go," said June.

Andy pulled up in front of the Berger household, he paused for a moment, in his mind's eye he could see Susan standing there waving him off on the nights he left after a visit and went back to his flat alone before she moved in.

As they approached the door the Berger brass nameplate stood out like a beacon to the former occupant.

"Hi Colin," said June as he answered the door

"Hello please come in," said Colin politely "thank you so much for coming so quickly"

Andy and June watched as Colin sat alone in his late brother s house and was shaking. Neither Andy nor June said anything initially. Andy had a gut feeling something was amiss and the dam was about to burst.

"Colin, you asked us here tonight is everything alright?" asked Andy

Colin stared at the television.

"No" he replied.

"There is something I want you both to see and this kills me to give you this," Colin handed Andy and June a couple of packages and several videos. "Please take them away I never want to see them again. Get justice for those kids please."

Andy and June did not know the significance of what they had been given at that time.

Despite being asked by Andy what the packages contained Colin explained that he was not wanting to detail the contents and on viewing and reading everything he had handed to them it would become clear.

"Colin this pales into insignificance for me but I have a jewellery box belonging to Susan. Rightfully it is part of her estate and should be with you."

"Andy keep it or do with it as you wish please, it is our gift to you from her."

"Thank you," replied Andy.

At that very second, the television which had been on with the volume set low turned grey and the announcer stated "We are unable to bring you tonight's programme due to legal reasons. We hope to air this programme at a future date, Diamond Investigates apologise for any inconvenience caused."

"Do you know what that was all about?" he asked.

"Yes," said Andy. "Seems the lawyers have managed to get the programme withdrawn, no doubt some major players are flexing their muscles."

Colin just nodded understanding what Andy meant. Andy and June rose from their seats and shook hands with Colin Berger and thanked him for his assistance as they were leaving the house. For Andy, this was the last time that he would visit the Berger household closing another chapter in his life.

As they sat in Andy's car he handed June the videos that he had been carrying.

"Your place or mine?" asked Andy

"Mine is closer" replied June "So let's go"

When they arrived at June's she invited Andy inside.

"Do you know this is the first time I have been in here?" said Andy.

"No, no way," she responded

"Yep. Let's get this done June," he said as he sat down beside her at a table

"Andy opened up the envelopes and found hundreds of photographs enough to get a mountain of convictions against everyone involved."

"June inserted a videotape then pressed the play button on her video recorder"

They watched as adults engaged in sexual acts with young girls and boys had been recorded between all those involved. These were not fixed cameras or secret recordings; these were created by someone actively recording and moving around the room with a video camera. Andy and June sat flabbergasted at what they were watching.

"What in the name of god do we do with this?" asked Andy

"I haven't a clue any more than I did the last time" replied June.

"Do you know what June I am going away for a few days I need away," as they gathered the evidence together.

"I will conceal this securely with the other stuff; we need to think about this June"

"Yes, I know that we do, just get it out of here please" she requested

Andy took what was given to them and took it home. He concealed everything with the previous items he had been given by Kerry. He knew that where they were was safe for the meantime. His thoughts were Crown Office direct, or David Diamond. He only trusted David now and of course, June.

Less than twenty-four hours later, Andy threw his bags onto the scales at the airport and watched as the uniformed lady monitored the weight in his case before wrapping the flight tag around the handle. She looked at Andy as she checked his passport and handed him his boarding pass.

"Enjoy your flight sir," she said as his bag disappeared behind her.

His small piece of hand luggage was slung over his shoulder as he wandered towards the duty-free area, where he took a brief look at what was on offer. Cigarettes were of no interest to him, so he chose a small bottle of after-shave initially followed by a fine bottle of brandy which he took to the counter and paid for in cash.

A few hours later, the familiar sight of Tenerife came into view as the plane hovered above the island waiting for a landing slot. This was Andy's home from home, a place he knew so well. He had friends on this island that he looked forward to seeing again.

Passing through passport control he collected his bag from the conveyer belt. He walked out into that familiar smell of the Tenerife air. He looked around as holidaymakers made their way to their buses ready to deposit them at their apartments and hotels all over the island. Those heading north had the longest journey. Opening the door of the white Mercedes taxi, throwing his bag into the rear seat, he said, "Apartmentos Santiago, Playa de Las Americas por favour."

"Si," said the driver as he spun the car out of the airport making his way onto the motorway heading south.

Following his late-night arrival, he booked into the apartments and collected the key to room 410, his room for the duration of his stay. Opening the door and putting the light on he looked around, twin-bedded room, immaculate condition, he observed before sliding open the balcony door giving him a sea view and expansive views over the area. The bright lights of the pubs and clubs twinkled in the night air. They were far enough away not to cause him annoyance or loss of sleep. The last twenty-four hours had taken its toll on Andy, his bags could wait to be unpacked in the morning as he had seven peaceful days to look forward to and put the trauma of the last few weeks behind him.

About seven o'clock the sunlight poured through the windows of his hotel room on the island, down in the southern part at Playa de Las Americas, Andy got up and went down to breakfast where he sat alone with his coffee looking about him observing the other guests. He went towards the reception and out the doors. He strolled along the seafront in his shorts and T-shirt, this is what is needed for the next seven days, time away from everything and everyone. he thought to himself. Alone with his thoughts, he stopped off at various bars in the Adeje Bajo area. A coffee here and there and a little snack.

Night-time brought a different perspective on the whole scene as the bars came alive with their flashing coloured lights attached to the walls outside. Waiters in their white shirts and black trousers, trays under their arms going from table to table. Cervezas y Cuba Libres being served to broken Spanish speaking customers with the usual gracias amigo from a customer being thrown in for good measure. Andy sat on a seat at the front of a bar. He watched the waves roll in towards him. They never stop no matter what happens in life. Everything goes on in life. The only ones that stop are those that are left behind.

As Andy went back to his hotel another late flight from Glasgow had arrived in what appeared to be a hen party for the blushing bride all out for a few days of madness. This was unusual as groups of females on hen weekends celebrating the forthcoming marriage of a bride usually stayed local to their abodes or frequented the local city centre, but something was different with this group of women. As Andy stood at the lift there were shouts from the females booking in at the reception in his direction which he chose to ignore. Andy of a few years ago would have been first to encourage them but not this time.

"Right girls leave him alone," said one of the party.

"I will for tonight but not tomorrow night," said another.

"Ding dong, king kong, he is mine before the weekend is over" another chipped in laughing.

"Hey big boy get it out for the girls" shouted the bride-to-be in a mock wedding outfit.

"I am so sorry for their behaviour," said a voice behind him awaiting the lift.

"Life goes on, we all need to have fun when we can Catherine" he replied without turning around.

"Yes, it does Andy, what are the chances of us being here at the same time?"

"It is just fate Catherine, just fate."

"How are you?" she asked.

"Not just now Catherine, you are here with your friends for a party weekend, by the looks of it, keep it that way, please."

"Hey, Catherine, you trying to get a head start on us with him" shouted one of the girls.

The doors to the lift finally opened and Andy stepped back to let Catherine in with her case. He joined her in the small lift. Floors 3 and 4 were chosen. As the lift rose, they said nothing to each other. On floor 3 Catherine got out.

"Goodnight Catherine," he said.

"Goodnight Andy," was her reply as the doors closed.

Andy's recent loss was still so raw given the circumstances and to have Catherine so close to him so many miles away from home was a comfort. They both had suffered losses of unimaginable proportions, now they had even more in common than ever before.

The following morning as he sat alone at breakfast with his thoughts of what might have been, he looked up from the table.

"Can I join you please?" asked Catherine

"Of course," he replied.

"When did you get here Andy?"

"Twenty-Four hours before you," he said as they sat opposite each other at breakfast.

"Hey, Catherine if you don't get into his pants today give me a shot at him."

"Sally behave please" replied Catherine shaking her head.

"Catherine the girls are here for fun frolics and mega amounts of drink for a few days they know nothing about me or us, so I am cool with it all honestly," said Andy, "go out, get pissed with your friends, have fun, that is why you are here. Do you know this is unusual I thought hen nights took place around the city not this far out of town?"

"Listen Andy the guy she is marrying is loaded, told her to choose her favourite destination and bingo we are all here at his expense. Normally it would be one night up the town but not for this guy."

"Wow, well make the best of it Catherine and, have a great time," he said as he stood up.

Andy left his table when one of the girls shouted at him "Hey big boy what is your name?"

Andy looked at Catherine as if seeking her approval to reveal his identity. Catherine smiled and nodded.

"Me?" he said looking around, "My name is Andy, Andy Blackmore" he replied going out the door.

Murmurs went around the room before one of the girls called over to Catherine,

"Catherine, is that your Andy Blackmore?"

"Right we are here to party, Andy was a long time ago so let it go please," she said.

"Yes, party time for breakfast might as well start early," said the bride as they headed for the bar. Catherine decided that this was not for her at this time of the morning and made the decision to return to her room to relax.

While sitting on the balcony of her room, overlooking the road leading up to the apartments, she watched Andy head out of the building alone and go towards the beach carrying his towel. Her head was in a spin. She was there for a hen weekend and had run into the only person she had ever loved in her entire life and nothing had changed for her. She had not been out with anyone since him. She still loved him deeply and she knew he still had something for her if their meeting a few weeks ago at the gym was anything to go by. She also had thoughts about him losing Susan and the effect that would have had on him as only weeks had gone by since her death. What has brought us together so far from home? If Susan had not died, he would not be here. If Susan had not died they would be together today, back in Scotland. If my pal was not getting married I would not be here. If my pal was not getting married, I would be at work, she thought to herself as she leaned forward lifting her glass of iced water which she sipped as the heat of the Canarian sunshine, warmed her white-painted balcony with its black ornate designed safety rail. Catherine was not a regular drinker or into the young heavy-duty madness that seemed to surround these nights even back home, never mind a weekend abroad. She thought that she was a bit "old" for all this and wanted something a bit more sedate, but she had accepted the invitation to be there. After a couple of hours on her balcony, she went downstairs and into the bar where she watched as the girls were downing shorts, tequila with salt and lemon was the order of the day. The Spanish waiters were lining up for the carnage that would undoubtedly follow, the clock headed for midday, the temperature began to rise as the sun crept towards its highest point.

"Hey, Catherine, are you here to party or what" shouted the bride.

"Yes, but I also value my kidneys and liver" she replied laughing "tell you what get me a lager, that shall do me just now."

As the party started to gather pace, they all went outside moving their drinks with them and commandeering a corner of the pool area. The girls were loud but orderly and giving the guys, single and married, a hard time of it as they passed by. There was a huge group huddle for a moment. The bride made a speech "What goes on tour stays on tour" a pact that was sealed as they joined hands in sisterhood. For Catherine, who had finished her drink slowly, it was to be a quiet walk to her room before going along the seafront and onto the beach as she slipped away from the group.

Wearing a long black flimsy sarong, which she had bought specifically for this trip, over her black bikini, she slipped her feet into her open-toed sandals. She tied her hair back into a ponytail. A beach towel and a book filled the cotton bag that she had kept for many a long year, way back to her hippie days of the late sixties and early seventies. She loved the multi-colours and the huge green marijuana leaf design, it was a link to her past, even though she had never tried drugs of any type, the bag was just symbolic of her era. An era that was filled with Love Peace and Music that culminated at Woodstock in 1969. That bag was like a travelling companion to her over the years, she knew, that when she got home, it would go into her suitcase ready for the next adventure if there ever was another one, as she was still alone and caring for her brother Barry. Locking the bedroom door at her back, she made her way from the third floor in the lift to the ground floor then out of the reception area, she could see the sea a few minutes' walk away from her.

As she wandered along the promenade she sat down at a small café and ordered a fresh orange juice. She looked over towards the sea and watched as couples, friends and family enjoyed the sunshine with the feeling of being free to do as they pleased. Older holidaymakers strolled along the promenade, hand in hand, arm in arm, some, she thought, seeing out their final years together. Those who were unable to walk were pushed in wheelchairs by loving and loyal wives and husbands, others, who had nobody, had their nursing home carers performing that duty. To someone like Catherine, who spent her life in a busy Accident and Emergency Unit at the local hospital day in and day out there was something tranquil about this whole scenario. Finishing her soft drink, she made her way down onto the beach which seemed strange to her, gone was the golden sands of other holidays to be replaced by the black volcanic ash Tenerife was famous for. Her bag over her shoulder, her sandals held in her other hand, she ran her toes through the black ash with an occasional dip into the blue waters to clean them, then catching the sight of a familiar figure leaving the sea and lying down on a sunbed not far from her.

"Is this sunbed free?" she asked.

"No Catherine it is not, I am with a famous actress who wants to remain anonymous, so go away."

"I think she has gone for a siesta." She replied

"Oh well, it is all yours then" he replied face down on the sunbed with the sun hitting his back.

Catherine sat next to Andy on the edge of the sunbed looking around her at the other sun worshipers. No matter what she thought she could not find the right words to begin her conversation with Andy.

Taking a deep breath, she plucked up the courage to ask Andy how he was feeling.

"At this time, I don't know what I feel, but having you here helps. For me, nothing ever changed between us if that is what you are getting at, it was just a case of the wrong place, wrong time, wrong everything, or things could have been so different."

"In what way?" She asked

"Well even though you are years and years older than me you would have had a younger husband by now and we could have been sailing the high seas together with a load of kids, but you binned your toyboy and the rest is history as they say," he said sitting up and looking at her with a smile on his face watching her closely from behind his sunglasses. They both laughed at that one as Andy held out his hand towards Catherine in friendship which she accepted in the same manner. As Andy lay back Catherine held onto his hand.

"Do you not have a party to attend?" he asked.

"Not at the moment" she replied "not at the moment" letting the sentence drift away

For Catherine, as she lay down on the sunbed opposite, the years went rolling back to her times with Andy, but knowing everything he had been through, and what he had just said to her, she had to tread carefully and be there for him as a friend.

Several hours later, Andy and Catherine got back to the hotel, the corner of the pool occupied by her friends was a scene of carnage as predicted with bottles and glasses lying everywhere. Some of the girls in the party were comatose beyond belief but the till kept ringing and the staff could not care less what state they were getting into as long as the money and the tips kept rolling in. Andy took off his t-shirt and threw his towel onto a vacant sunbed by the side of the pool then slipping into the water to cool down, as Catherine walked towards her friends.

"Wooohooo, where have you guys been" was getting shouted.

"On the beach," said Catherine as she surveyed the scene.

"Go get a drink there is loads of money in the kitty" shouted the bride.

"I think I shall pass on this one and start after dinner."

"I am heading upstairs Catherine thank you for today," said Andy leaning on the edge of the pool looking up at her.

"You are welcome, Andy."

"You girls have fun tonight, and take care out there." She looked at Andy as he disappeared under the water to the other side of the pool where he lifted himself out of the water and retrieved his t-shirt and towel before going into the reception area. Catherine rounded up the girls and got them safely upstairs and into their rooms. Some would not see dinner or Saturday night out on the town.

After he showered and got into his casual evening clothes, wearing a white short-sleeved shirt, sky blue jeans and trainers Andy made his way to the dining area of the apartments. Catherine was sitting with what remained of her party having her dinner. With the number of empty seats around her, the sunshine and alcohol had claimed a few victims which brought a wry smile from Andy who was by a now a veteran visitor to the island and knew the breeze from the sea hid the true temperature. As Catherine and what remained of the party were leaving the dining room she saw him sitting alone, and approached his table.

"Hey, are you okay?"

"Yes of course I am, thank you" he replied.

"Well I am sure if you want to join a hen party the girls would make you more than welcome," she said with a smile.

"Em, I think that I shall give that suggestion a big thank you for the offer, and an even bigger no thank you," he said laughing.

"Well don't you go home and say you were not asked" was her jovial response.

"Catherine, where are you guys going tonight?" asked Andy

"Oh, someplace called, what is it called again, ah, yeah, Veronicas, one of the girls knows it she was here last year"

Andy looked at Catherine and nodded slowly. "Do me a favour, keep an eye on them, and in particular yourself please"

"Yeah sure," she said wondering what he meant by that comment and the way he had delivered it.

"Catherine lets go" came the shout from the reception area

"Seeya," said Catherine

"Yeah sure thing, enjoy yourself please" was his reply as he watched Catherine leave while finishing his dinner.

Later that night Andy walked passed the 'Patch' a well-known area in Playa de Las Americas for its discos and bars. Near to that area were bars dedicated to their nation. Linekers was popular with the English and The Highlander was popular with the Scots there was little to no animosity in that area despite their rivalry, The Dubliner was self-explanatory. This was not Ibiza or Majorca this was a more laid back, island. Dedicated bars were not Andy's scene at all. He was more a traditional type of person who had been to the island many times before, so he had contacts there, as he wandered into his favourite bodega.

"Hola Miguel," said Andy.

"Hola Andy Como Esta mi amigo?" as they wrapped their arms around each other kissing each other on each cheek.

"Muy Bien gracias"

"Y tu?"

"Si muy bien"

"Tu familia Miguel?"

"Si Muy bien gracias"

"Una cerveza grande Miguel por favor"

"Si, mi amigo"

"When did you get back here Andy?" Miguel asked.

"Yesterday to be truthful" he replied, "I have something to tell you."

Miguel had been his friend of many years travelling to the island sat with him at a table overlooking the beach and listening to the waves, Andy told Miguel what had happened back in Scotland. He had never met Susan, but Andy had planned to bring her out in the summer to meet him and his family. He also told Miguel about Catherine being on the island at this time and that they were together years ago.

"Andy, mi amigo, my friend. Este es el Destino, Susan ha planeado esto desde lejos,"

"Which translated means what, Miguel?" asked Andy

"This is fate Susan has planned this from afar, she is deciding your destiny she wants you to be happy".

"With Catherine or someone else?"

"Si con Catarina"

"Gracias mi amigo," said Andy staring into his glass

"I had to come all the way here to get the peace I got here tonight Miguel, gracias. "Hasta Mañana mi amigo," he said as he left the small bar.

As Andy took a slow sombre walk through the streets passing the 'Patch' or 'Veronicas' the hub of Las Americas, he saw the lights flashing colourfully and the arrows flashing pointing patrons to the doorways into the clubs awaiting the full swing of summer and all the madness that would bring from June to September or October school week, then the pubs, clubs and restaurants would close down on the island for a few months so they had to make their money to survive the winter.

As he looked towards The Dubliner Bar, an icon in the area, he decided to go in there. They served the best Guinness on the whole island. They also had the best bands playing until two in the morning before they closed at three o'clock. This was a favourite pub of his for many years.

As usual, it was chaos, with loads of Irish and other nationalities. Even early in the year, this was the pub to be in, during the summer it was a tight squeeze when a band took the stage. Everyone knew this was the place to be.   Pint of Guinness please Andy shouted over the noise. The band were blaring out songs from the island of Ireland plus songs from the charts and some heavy metal.

"Andy, Andy, Andy," shouted a female voice. Looking over at the female waving her arms in his direction he had no idea who she was, "I am Brenda and we are queuing up to shag you, Andy, Catherine is over there."

Andy looked over at her "Brenda even if I tried, I could not keep up with you lot" he called back.

She burst out laughing.

"Hiya," said a relatively sober Catherine as she stood next to him at the bar in a tight white dress and flat shoes.

"Hiya," said Andy.

"Have you had a good night out?" she asked.

"I went and saw a friend of mine that has a pub here and had a long chat with him."

"What about you, I see it is still going strong although the numbers have been reduced."

"Yeah there was a few that failed to start the night, casualties as we would say"

"How did you find this place," said Catherine

"I have been here many times over the past few years there is nothing I don't know about this island would you like to see it?"

"Are you asking me out again Andy Blackmore thousands of miles from home?"

Andy looked at Catherine "Este es el Destino Susan ha planeado Esto Desde lejos" kept running through his head time and time again.

"Catherine you are here on a special weekend with your friends, I cannot do that"

"Yes, you can and if you are, I want to go" she replied looking at him

"Okay, I would love to take you around this island"

"I accept your invitation," she said pausing "but, as a mate, a friend, someone there for you at this time"

 Andy nodded, took her hand in his giving it a little squeeze. "Hasta luego Catarina"

"Whatever that means sure thing" she replied as Andy finished his Guinness and about to leave the pub alone.

"Andy are you heading for the hotel?" shouted Catherine over the noise of the band.

"Yes," he replied with a nod of his head.

"Can I walk with you if I go get my bag?"

"Yes, you can" he replied

As they walked along the promenade away from Veronicas the prom got quieter. Couples walked by hand in hand. Waiters had finished their shifts. Waitresses headed home and for the buses which ran into the small hours of the morning at this time of the year. This island had a special feel about it Andy felt at home here for some strange reason, it was so laid back.

The grey paving stones were spotless, people respected the cleanliness of the island even where the teens gathered for fun there were loads of rubbish bins which were used.

The African "lookie" men were plying their trade selling fake watches to drunken young tourists who had bartered a good price if there was such a thing as a good price. Other 'lookie lookies' were on the look-out for the local police in this game of cat and mouse. When the whistle came 'lookie lookies' jumped onto the beach concealing themselves behind the wall until the police car passed by. African women were plaiting hair for teenage tourists while watching over the others who were active prostitutes working to survive. The night had come alive for the Africans.

"Can we sit here Andy?"

"Yes of course"

They sat next to each other on a bench on the promenade in silence, listening to the waves crashing onto the beach and ending their lives having started way out somewhere in the sea then rolling back.

"Right there is something I have to ask you Andy and I am being serious," said Catherine followed by a hiccup.

"Okay," said Andy suspecting the drink she had consumed was starting to take effect.

With a slight slur in her speech, Catherine said to Andy that she had never been on Tenerife before and there was something that she, really had to know.

"Okay when you are ready, so am I," replied Andy

"What is, what is a lookie lookie man," she asked followed by another hiccup

Andy stifled the laughter that was building up inside him "Okay" he replied shaking his head, "A lookie, lookie man is the African guys that you see standing about on the prom"

"Right" she replied.

"So, they will come up to you, show you watches, chains, bracelets, and say, lookie, lookie, then try to charge you a fortune for rubbish"

"Right" she replied, "now I know"

"Please come with me," said Andy

"Where?"

"Down here" as he led the way

Andy took off his shoes he did not wear socks. Catherine took off her shoes also. He held an outstretched hand taking her right hand in his left hand and led her to the edge of the water. They felt the water lap over their feet as they stood there for a while listening to the surf. "Come on let's go," he said. As they walked at the edge of the waves, along the beach, hand in hand, they talked about years gone by that they missed together.

Andy also bared his soul to Catherine about Susan, his engagement, his plans, he stopped short of saying she had been murdered by her father. He also let everything rip about his feelings for her and how it was so different from Susan.

"Thank you, Andy," said Catherine

"For what?"

"Your honesty," she said

"I now know where I stand at the moment"

"Where is that Catherine?"

"Hopefully by your side, I cannot and never will replace Susan, I just want to be Catherine"

"Can we sit here together on the sand please?" she asked

"Yes," said Andy

"Listen, listen to the water, is that not the most beautiful sound in the world" as she wrapped her arms around her legs that she had pulled up resting her chin on her knees.

"Yes, it is, always has been to me out here," said Andy.

"Strange that fate has brought us here."

"There is something I have wanted to tell you for a long long time, Andy."

"Do you remember when you asked me out."

"Yes."

"Did you know that I could not go because of Barry."

"Initially, no"

"Well, Barry is still with me."

"Okay."

"Right listen to me as the waves roll in please and say nothing" Catherine paused for a moment.

"Andy you have no idea how much I loved you back then, I still love you now just the way I did then when you and your colleagues ruined my family. I hated you and them, but at the end of the day, Eric was responsible. I was there in court the day he was given thirty years imprisonment or whatever he got, I was also there when the kid was jailed, and I felt a bit sorry for him, but he did what he did. Andy, it was me that decided to end us, nobody else, not you, not anyone else just me and to this day I sorely regret it. I knew that you and Susan had got together, and I was pleased for you. I knew that you had got engaged and I was pleased that you had found someone special in your life after us. I knew that Susan had been killed in that awful accident and my heart went out to you."

They both sat on the beach listening to the surf for a few moments.

"Well Catherine this is where you and I level the playing field," said Andy.

"Sandra Berger who would have been my future mother-in-law was murdered." He paused

"Sheena Gough, who I knew, was murdered." He paused again

"Susan Berger, who I loved dearly, was murdered." He paused again delivering one line at a time

"They were all murdered by Brian Berger husband and father. Brian Berger who would have been my future father-in-law committed suicide. What I can tell you is that the police are covering all this up," then he fell silent.

"Can I ask why?" She enquired.

"Yes, but at this time I cannot tell you, Catherine."

"What shall go public soon will shock you I shall see to that."

Andy stood up and pulled Catherine up off the sand, they walked back to the hotel together.

"Key 305 please," said Catherine to the hotel security at the reception desk.

"Key 410 for me please," said Andy.

"La clave 410," said the security officer handing Andy his key.

"La clave 305 no está aquí, lo siento."

"What is he saying."

"He said that your key is not here he is sorry."

"Shit, door banging night then for me."

"Don't be silly I have a key," he said holding up his room key

"No way," said Catherine.

"Okay, goodnight as he walked over to the lift and pushed the lift call button."

"Are you going to leave me here?" she asked looking in his direction

"Yep, goodnight Catherine." As he entered the lift and the door closing behind him.

She watched the lift go to the fourth floor with the security guard watching her. She swallowed her pride and pressed the call button. 0 showed on the indicator and the door opened. "410 in case you have forgotten," said Andy with a smile standing in the lift.

As the lift ascended to the fourth floor Andy asked Catherine a question which stunned her.

"See before it all went pear-shaped for us would you have married me if I had asked you?"

Catherine hesitated before replying "Yes"

Andy opened the door to the twin-bedded room. "The one near the window is mine you can have the other one," he said.

"Thanks, Andy" she replied.

When Catherine awoke Andy was gone. She went down to the dining room where she was greeted by her friends who looked the worse for wear from the night before. "Before you say or think anything nothing happened," said Catherine. Howls of derision met that comment.

"What about you lot did you all behave."

"Yes, we did we were good girls well some of us were," said the bride-to-be.

"Catherine," said Brenda looking over at the door and nodding to where Andy was standing.

Catherine walked over to the door.

"I forgot to ask you, when are you going home?"

"We have tonight then fly back tomorrow."

"Have you anything planned for today?" asked Andy.

"By the looks of this lot, more drinking, why?"

"Well if you wish I can give you a quick tour of the island before I return this hire car, I have got us."

"I would love that to be honest, not really into this drinking lark anyway."

"Girls would you mind if I went out with Andy for a while" she shouted to her friends.

"Of course, not Catherine you go enjoy yourself we shall catch up later."

"Okay, I shall be back for dinner at eight o'clock." She said as she left the dining room.

As they set off Andy headed for the motorway that would take them from Las Americas towards Los Gigantes and Puerto de Santiago. Onwards to the Icod de Los Vinos, then stopping for lunch in the northern part of the island at Puerto De La Cruz. Andy had been there many years before, but it had grown and changed so much.

"This island is so beautiful," said Catherine.

"So is the company I have today," said Andy.

As they drove into the Orotava Valley Catherine marvelled at the greenery surrounding her before going into the Parque National de Las Canadas de Tiede.

Andy explained to Catherine that this area had been used to make scenes from the films One Million Years BC and Planet of the Apes.

They stood gazing over the bare valley which was such a contrast compared to the Orotava Valley.

As they drove down the east coast Andy said he wanted to show Catherine somewhere special. Soon thereafter they arrived in the small village of Candelaria. Catherine stared at the most beautiful small white chapel she had ever seen. As they went in, she lit a candle and placed it onto a holder. As Andy went to do the same Catherine stopped him placing her hand on his "That candle was for Susan" she said.

"We are now in the Basílica de Nuestra Señora de Candelaria isn't it so peaceful," said Andy.

"The guys outside are Guanchos who guard this place, I believe that is the story."

Andy was not the religious sort by any means, but this little house of god brought much peace to him due to its sheer beauty.

"Would you like a drink of some sort?" He asked quietly.

"Yes please," said replied

"C'mon then follow me."

Within a few minutes, they sat outside a small cafe

"Hola, Buenos tardes," said the waitress

"Hola, Buenos tardes senora, por favor, dos cafe con leche," said Andy asking for two coffees with milk.

"Gracias senor," she replied noting their order.

"Do you know something?" said Catherine.

"This is my first time on this island, and I have fallen in love."

"That is good I am pleased hopefully it is as much as I love it," said Andy.

"Catherine when I retire, I plan to retire to this island. Candelaria is a beautiful place, unspoiled by the tourism of the south, but, close enough to get there when I want to and visit Miguel and his family."

Having finished their coffees, they set off again, heading south and towards Los Cristianos passing through small villages that are missed out on the main tourist routes. About seven-thirty that evening, some nine hours after they left the hotel Andy dropped off the car at the hiring agent and completed the relevant paperwork. He and Catherine walked the short distance back to the hotel.

Much noise was heard from the pool area from the hen party and Catherine's friends when they entered the reception area

"Thank you so much for today," Catherine said as she kissed Andy's cheek.

"You are very welcome, now, I have kept you from your friends long enough today."

"Oh, by the sounds of things I haven't missed much, I think I shall go to the room for a little while."

"Maybe see you later then," said Andy as she got out the lift on the third floor and Andy on the fourth floor.

Andy went to his room where he poured himself a local brandy and sat out on the balcony with its two small white chairs and a table. The view over the sea was Andy's favourite part of his breaks out there.

As he sat there looking back on his day out with Catherine and everything that had gone on over the past couple of weeks, he closed his eyes until there was a knock on the door to his room. Slowly he rose from his seat and opened the door.

"Andy can I come in and sit for a little while please," said Catherine looking a little embarrassed.

"Eh, why? I thought you were going to your room?"

"Well, its em, currently in use shall I say."

"Oh well, would you like a drink, I have brandy available."

"Yes, that would be nice" she replied.

"I have something to tell you, something I need to speak to you about, Andy."

"Yeah, sure no problem" he replied as he poured her a brandy and sat down at the opposite side of the small table from her.

"After we split up, or should I say after I ended everything, Barry refused to speak to me for weeks and weeks because he thought you were his friend and I had sent you away and you never came back to see him and he blamed me for all that. He still remembers you."

"Catherine don't beat yourself up over us parting please you can't continue doing that."

"I do and seeing you again has brought it all back."

"Well for now and forever we shall be friends," said Andy.

"Catherine, I know that you are up there I can hear your voice. Room available again girl." Came the shout from below them.

"Who is that" whispered Andy.

"Brenda, you had a lucky escape," she said leaving Andy's room.

Catherine went into her room and looked around "Brenda what has been going on in here looking at the state of the place"

"Awe Catherine that was awesome wae him I can tell you; I will clean up"

"Awesome with who?"

"Pedro, the young barman"

"Brenda you be lucky if he is eighteen you are over forty and married"

"I am forty for your information and he was like a stallion it just wouldn't go down"

"Oh well I hope you don't live to regret it," said Catherine.

"As long as everyone says nothing it will be fine, what goes on tour stays on tour."

"Who else is at it?"

"A few have been active since we got here and if I get half a chance, he is mine again later."

"How has your day been Catherine?"

"Really lovely thank you now get yourself sorted out"

Andy sat with a broad smile on his face as he realised Catherine and Brenda were unaware that their conversation could be overheard as the patio doors were wide open onto their balcony.

Catherine went and sat on the balcony alone while Brenda tidied up the bedroom and went for a shower. She sat with the drink Andy had poured her in his room that she had carried downstairs. Her thoughts drifted to the wonderful day that she had spent with him as they went around the island seeing the sights that the tourists miss as they head for the bars and clubs interspersed with a hamburger or hot dog to keep them going. "Oh hell, oh hell," she thought to herself as she thought back to what she said at the small cafe in Candelaria. I said I had fallen in love when sitting at the table with him she thought. Oh, I need to straighten that out with him as she swallowed her drink and went to her bag where she opened a bottle of wine and poured herself a large red.

As she entered the dining room she went straight over to a table where Andy was sitting alone and taking a deep breath she said, "Andy Blackmore, it is nine o'clock on a Sunday night in Playa de Las Americas, Tenerife, we are thousands of miles away from home and this afternoon when we were sitting having a coffee in a cafe in Candelaria I

174

said that I had fallen in love what I meant was that I had fallen in love with this island and I hope that you did not take it the wrong way that I had fallen in love with you all over again because I can't do that as I have never fallen out of love with you in the first place and I know that you have just been through a traumatic time in your life and this is the wrong time and place for us to meet again and everything that I am saying is coming out wrong and see if in time you let me back into your life again I will marry you if you ask me"

Looking up at Catherine, he leaned back casually, put down his knife and fork and scratched his chin as Catherine stared intently at him breathing heavily.

"Catherine, take a breath as you got through that in one breath at some speed," he said, "Secondly have you been drinking since we got back? Thirdly this whole dining room is looking in this direction in silence even the waiters have stopped serving meals wondering what the hell is going on."

"If you look to your right all your mates are at that table looking over at you, this is like a scene from a mad girly slapstick film"

"So, what is your answer Andy," asked Catherine.

"I have forgotten the question," replied Andy

"Can you forgive what I did, and can we get back together when you are ready?"

Andy looked at Catherine, "I need time please but yes I think we can. We can get back again but that is a long time away now"

As the place erupted into applause the head waiter placed a bottle of white wine on his table

Catherine's friends cheered loudly and one shouted "That is him off-limits tonight girls"

Andy reached out his hand and held Catherine's. "Thank you, you have made being here easy," he said looking at her with a smile.

Catherine walked over and joined her friends at their table and the place got back to normal. After dinner, the girls went on into the town for the last time and there was no doubt it was going to be a night to remember or forget for them. Catherine decided to join her friends for one last fling out on the 'Patch'. Andy watched as they all left together, knowing this could be a night of carnage.

Later that evening he made his way to his favourite, small local bodega, but slightly off the beaten track. Squeezed between all the modern-day pubs lay a small bodega that had been there long before Playa De Las Americas became a popular tourist attraction. Nowadays, it was owned by Miguel Gonzalez, his friend, a small, slightly built man, with sharp features and dark brown eyes. His dark tanned skin set off his Canarian appearance. Miguel was the third generation to own the bodega. It was handed over to him by his father who occupied a small table every day at the far end of the premises away from the midday sun and the growing nightlife. In all the years' Andy had been frequenting the bodega nothing had changed. The oak beams on the ceiling that looked like they had come from a Spanish galleon, the brick bar with its original dark timber top, the gantry was similar, there were no measures like there was in Glasgow pubs. A measure was three ice cubes or when you said "stop" to stop the glass overflowing. Dark tiles on the floor made cleaning easy. Tables, they appeared homemade in heavy oak timber, finding a level bit to balance the glass was a challenge, but this was the real Tenerife and Andy loved that. Like, at home "Me Casa" had its 'locals' the guys who would be there night after night. Andy was a 'local' for seven or fourteen nights, twice a year, and he was known by the Canarians who frequented "Me Casa."

It was about 1973 or 1974, when Andy was working on the building sites as a bricklayer, he was making a lot of money, more than his mates were making and he had already caught the travel bug having travelled to a few countries in Europe. While his mates were heading for Blackpool and Scarborough, he ventured out to Tenerife on his own. One day he was walking through the narrow streets when he came upon a man outside a bodega trying to repair some brickwork that looked centuries old. He held a trowel in one hand and some cement lay on the ground on a bit of plywood. It was almost archaic, Andy watched as he struggled with the job. Andy's' lack of Spanish and the man's lack of English resulted in sign language resulting in the man handing Andy the trowel. He watched as Andy pointed the brickwork to perfection within half an hour. Andy's pay was a pint of lager, but, more importantly, years of friendship, Spanish to English lessons, English to Spanish lessons and a lot of laughs followed along the way.

"Bueno mi amigo que hay de Catarina," asked Miguel asking how Catherine was.

"Ella es Buena gracias" Andy replied telling Miguel that she was well.

"So, Andy you gonna see her again when you get home?" asked Miguel.

"Miguel, I need time to get over my loss before starting over again."

"Si entiendo, I understand." He replied

"It is always nice to sit here with you my friend," said Andy.

"and you also Andy maybe someday you come to live here"

"Do you know something that would be beautiful."

"Y Catarina?"

"Now that has to be seen and for the future, I can't even think about that just now," Andy replied.

They sat chatting for a while outside as the heat of the evening decreased. Andy finished his glass of lager before standing up from his table. "Miguel, Buenos tardes mi amigo, hasta mañana."

"Si mi amigo hasta mañana." Miguel watched as his friend wandered down the hill towards the 'Patch" for once he was concerned about him as he lifted the glasses from the table.

As Andy passed by the 'Patch' he stopped and leaned on a rail overlooking the clubs and pubs. He watched as the girls and the guys lurched from pub to pub, some not even making the next pub as their friends picked them up off the street as they unceremoniously unloaded their alcohol intake into the gutter. Couples left the clubs, and some headed for the sunbeds on the beach under the cover of darkness whether they were married or not with loved ones at home. Some, if not a lot, would live to regret this holiday away as the stories filtered back to the UK. White Mercedes taxis carried the walking wounded away from the venues to their flats and hotels in the surrounding areas as Andy caught sight of Catherine's group of friends. They had become a fragmented group which was not good as safety was in numbers with the amount of alcohol that was being consumed.

Andy scanned the groups he could see when he caught sight of Catherine with a few others. He watched as she appeared to be in a heated discussion with a male outside a club on the pavement. The floodlights shone down from the club giving him a good view of the scene. The incident was raging on as Catherine held onto Brenda who seemed the worse for wear.

"Excuse me do you speak English?" asked Andy as Catherine looked on saying nothing.

"Better than you ya Scottish prick."

"You seem to be annoying a couple of my friends."

"Who do you think you are Jock."

"Well for a start my name is not Jock, secondly, the ladies you are annoying are friends of mine."

"Piss off asshole they are going with me to my flat."

"For what reason?"

"For what reason," he asked as the pain shot from his groin right through his body.

"With what, no use to them now mate" as Andy grabbed and squeezed the Englishman's testicles within a fraction of destruction.

"Now my English friend," Andy said casually "this is with love from me to you."

"Right ladies taxi time," he said as he led them away.

"Andy what have you done to him," said Catherine.

"Oh, just tweaked a little nerve he shall be fine soon" as he looked at the male lying on the ground curled upwards and his hands between his legs.

"I shall watch out for the rest of your mates, get her back to the apartments, I shall be here."

Andy watched over the area for Catherine's mates, he was aware of what went on in this area. His eyes were everywhere as he saw the bridesmaid leaving with two young males and head for the beach. The African "lookie lookie" boys were everywhere making their money from the drunks.

"This is mental," said Catherine a short time later placing her hand on his shoulder.

"Why did you come back?" he asked with a furrowed brow.

"Because I want to spend my last night on this island with you and I don't mean sexually."

"C'mon, I want you to meet someone if he is still around" taking her hand as he led her through a few narrow streets.

"Miguel, Catarina," said Andy as Miguel began to close the bodega for the night.

"Encantado"

"He is charmed," said Andy.

"Lo siento, apologising, I forget you do not speak Spanish," said Miguel with a smile "I am so pleased to meet you Andy tells me about you lots."

"Oh, what did he tell you, Miguel?" Catherine asked

"Oh, he loved you very much from another time."

"Wrong answer Miguel," said Andy as he leaned forward burying his head in his hands.

"No Andy you say that to me," he said smiling not realising what he had said.

"Yes, Miguel but you are not supposed to tell her that."

"Okay, he does not tell me he loved you a lot."

"Geezuz this is getting like a scene from Fawlty Towers," said Andy.

"Yeah but I love it," said Catherine laughing.

"You know I love Faulty Towers Andy; I learn my English from that," said Miguel laughing.

"Hey, I give you a treat from here Cortado leche leche es a coffee."

Miguel came back with a tray, three small brandies, three small coffees, coffee in the centre of two kinds of milk.

"Your Andy he loves this, and he only gets this here on this island."

"So, My Andy loves this."

The significance of the wording 'my Andy' was not lost on him.

"Si señorita, mucho."

Catherine sipped her first Cortado leche leche coffee. "That is sweet and amazing."

Andy looked at her and smiled.

"Another little part of this island has got you then" Andy bowed his head shyly.

"I don't want you to go home tomorrow," he said looking at her.

"I have to, I have to get Barry and I shall be back at work before you get back."

The warmth of the night air surrounded them as they chatted with Miguel at the small table. Eventually, Andy decided that it was time for him and Catherine to return to their apartments.

"Miguel, mi amigo, gracias por el cafe y brandy Buenos noches."

"Goodnight Miguel so nice to meet you," Catherine said as she got ready to leave for the last time.

Miguel beckoned her close and whispered, "Marry mi amigo por favor."

"I hope so Miguel and we shall return here soon hopefully." She said looking at Miguel and nodding in his direction.

The white Mercedes taxi stopped outside the Santiago Apartments and Andy paid the small fare before they got out. They went into the reception area and collected their keys handed over by the late-night security guard. This time he had keys for both.

"Goodnight Catherine"

"Goodnight Andy enjoy the rest of your break."

"It's only a few days after you get back when I get back."

"Am I going to see you?" she asked.

"As a friend, and let's see how we go from there if that is okay" he replied.

"If it takes the rest of time, I shall wait I am not going to make the same mistake twice."

At midday, Andy watched from his balcony as the bus arrived to take the girls back to Glasgow after their few days of madness and a wedding pending at the weekend coming. He wondered if some of them would be sober enough to make it on time. He watched as Brenda took her secret back to the matrimonial home. He watched as the brides' mother took her night of madness on the beach with the two young bucks onto the bus with her. He watched as Catherine put her bag onto the pavement for the driver to load into the baggage area. Some of the girls were talking intently to her. Catherine stepped onto the bus without a glance around her, within seconds she stepped off again and looked up to the fourth floor, room 410.

"Hey Blackmore, will you be my partner at a wedding on Saturday" she shouted

Andy paused briefly before answering, "Yes Catherine, as your friend, I would be honoured"

"Thank you" she replied as she got on the bus for a second time. Andy watched as the bus pulled out of the apartments car park heading for the airport and a flight back to Glasgow.

For Andy, the next few days were an anti-climax. He shared moments with his friend Miguel and his wife Abril a name which Andy loved as she was born in April and named after that month. Andy spent his last night on the island with Miguel and Abril before returning to his apartment and packing his bags ready for the flight back to Glasgow. He looked out of the window as the plane rose effortlessly into the air and circled the island that he loved so much from the Reina Sofia Airport. The south was clear as the plane rose high revealing the West, North and East of the island before heading towards Spain, France, Ireland, coming in over Paisley and landing at Glasgow airport. Andy could have piloted this aircraft he knew the route so well.

What kept him smiling was that he was going home, back to where he started a couple of years ago, back to people he could trust, back to June and Joe and the rest of the team and more importantly Sergeant Black, his lord and mentor, with his secondment behind him. He was returning to Bankvale just over six months older, but years wiser.

Then there was Catherine and a wedding pending, he asked himself was it too soon after the death of Susan or had his life to go on without her?

Glossary of Terms

Bail / Bailed - Released from the police office or court to appear at court on a later date.

Bar Officer - A Police Officer who oversees the daily working of the police office during his shift accepting prisoners into the office, logging property, general prisoner care.

Bothy - A small hut or cottage

CID - Criminal Investigation Department

Circle the Wagons - Figure of speech for everyone to close ranks around a colleague to protect him or her.

Close – Entrance to a tenement in Glasgow

Crime - A crime is generally at common law against the person, murder, assault, rape etc.

Detained - Being kept for a specific time limit for lawful enquiry but not under arrest

Locus - The place where a crime or offence was committed

Muster/Muster Room - A gathering or assemble of people coming together for a common purpose / the meeting place

Offence – An example would be, Public Order Offences, generated by Acts of Parliament.

Probation - A sentence handed down by a court as an alternative to jail

Probationer - In this series, it refers to a new police officer who has to serve a two-year probation period before being confirmed in the rank of Constable

Station Constable - Similar role to the bar officer but with additional duties throughout the office

Suits / Soft Shoe Brigade - Complaints and Discipline Department, Senior police officers, so named because of their mode of dress

Suspect - A person suspected of committing a crime or offence

Tin Pail - Rhyming Slang for Jail

Turnkey - Usually a civilian employee sometimes a police officer charged with the care of prisoners, the origin is, turning the key

Drug Terms - Weed/Marijuana - Smack/Heroin - Coke/Cocaine

Worthies - Usually a group of local older unemployed residents known for their drinking sessions, can also be used for low-level local criminals, but also one worthy of praise.

Japanese Phrases

Karategi … Formal Japanese name for the suit used in competition or practice

Dojo … The room or the hall where martial arts are practised

Sensei … A teacher

Kata … A system of training exercises in karate or other martial arts

Ranking of Police Officers

Con … Constable

Sgt … Sergeant

Insp … Inspector

Ch. Insp … Chief Inspector

Supt … Superintendent

Chief Supt … Chief Superintendent

ACC … Assistant Chief Constable

Dep. Ch. Con … Deputy Chief Constable

Ch. Con… Chief Constable

About the Author

Born in the northeast of Scotland Simpson moved to Glasgow in the late 1950s spending his formative years in the East-end of Glasgow. His working life was spent in the civil service, forming life-long friendships with those in the Emergency Services. It was those friendships and a love of writing that led him to create this series while he enjoys the quiet life he returned to in the northeast of Scotland.

The Secondment

Other Books by this Author

For The Latest Information On

Available Novels

New Releases

&

Coming Soon

From this Author

Please Visit

JasamiPublishingLtd.com

Printed in Poland
by Anazon Fulfillment
Poland Sp. z o.o., Wrocław

64966852R00117